"Let's talk about you."

"Fine," Rafe said, his head whirling. Did sperm live for a full day? He was pretty sure it was possible…but the odds weren't on his side.

Weren't on his side? Was he mad? He should have been relieved. He didn't really want to be a father, did he? *Did* he?

He looked at Isabel and realized he did. With her, anyway.

The realization took his breath away.

He reefed his eyes away and stared down at the pool. Stared and stared and stared. And then his eyes flung wide. Who would have believed it?

"Rafe? Rafe, what's wrong? You look like you've seen a ghost or something."

Secret Passions

by
Miranda Lee

Desire changes everything!

Book One:
A Secret Vengeance
March (#2236)
The price of passion is...revenge

Book Two:
The Secret Love-Child
April (#2242)
The price of passion is...a baby

Miranda Lee

THE SECRET LOVE-CHILD

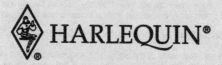

HARLEQUIN®

TORONTO • NEW YORK • LONDON
AMSTERDAM • PARIS • SYDNEY • HAMBURG
STOCKHOLM • ATHENS • TOKYO • MILAN • MADRID
PRAGUE • WARSAW • BUDAPEST • AUCKLAND

ISBN 0-373-12242-X

THE SECRET LOVE-CHILD

First North American Publication 2002.

Copyright © 2002 by Miranda Lee.

CHAPTER ONE

'PLEASE, Rafe. My reputation for reliability is on the line here.'

Rafe sighed. Les had to be really desperate to ask him to do this. His ex-partner knew full well the one job he'd hated when they'd been in the photographic business together was covering weddings. Where Les enjoyed the drama and sentiment of the bride and groom's big day, Rafe found the whole wedding scenario irritating in the extreme. The pre-ceremony nerves got on *his* nerves, as did all the hugging and crying that went on afterwards.

Rafe was not a big fan of women weeping.

On top of that, it was impossible to be seriously creative when the criterion was simply to capture every single moment of the day on film, regardless. Rafe, the perfectionist, had loathed having to work with the possibilities that the weather might be rotten, the settings difficult and the bridal party hopelessly unphotogenic.

As a top-flight fashion and magazine photographer, Rafe now had control over everything. The sets. The lighting. And above all...the models. When you shot a wedding, you had control over very little.

'I presume you can't get anyone else,' Rafe said, resignation in his voice.

'The wedding's on Saturday, exactly a fortnight from

today,' Les explained. 'You know how popular Saturday weddings are. Every decent photographer in Sydney will already be booked.'

'Yeah. Yeah. I understand. Okay, so what do you want me to do?'

'The bride's due at your place at noon today.'

Rafe's eyes flicked to the clock on the wall. It was eleven fifty-three. 'And what if I'd refused?'

'I knew you wouldn't let me down. You might be the very devil with women, but you're a good mate.'

Rafe shook his head at this back-handed compliment. So he'd had quite a few girlfriends over the years. So what? He was thirty-three years old, a better-than-average-looking bachelor who spent his days photographing bevies of beautiful women, a lot of whom were also single. It was inevitable that their ready availability, plus his active libido, would keep the wheels turning where his relationships were concerned.

But he wasn't a womaniser. He had one girlfriend at a time, and he never lied or cheated. He just didn't want marriage. Or children. Was that a crime? It seemed to be in some people's eyes.

Rafe wished his married friends—like Les—would understand that not everyone wanted the same things out of life.

'Just give me some details before the bride actually arrives,' he said a tad impatiently, 'so I won't look a right Charlie.'

'Okay, her name is Isabel Hunt. She's thirtyish, blonde and beautiful.'

'Les, you think *all* your brides are beautiful,' Rafe said drily.

'And so they are. On the day. But this one is beautiful all the time. You're going to enjoy photographing Ms Hunt, I promise you. Or should I say, Mrs Freeman. The lucky girl is marrying Luke Freeman, the only son and heir of Lionel Freeman.'

'Is that supposed to mean something to me? Who the hell is Lionel Freeman, anyway?'

'Truly, Rafe, you're a complete philistine when it comes to subjects other than food, the Phantom and photography. Lionel Freeman was one of Sydney's most awarded architects. Poor chap was killed in a car accident a couple of weeks back, along with his wife, so tread easily with the groom when you finally meet him.'

'Poor bloke. What rotten luck.' Rafe's own father had been killed in a car crash when Rafe had been only eight. It had been a difficult time in his life, one he didn't like dwelling on.

'Oh-oh. I just heard a car pull up outside. The bride-to-be, I gather, and right on time. I hope she's just as punctual on her wedding day. Now what about money, Les? What do you charge for a wedding these days?'

'A lot less than you could command, my friend. But I'm afraid you'll have to settle for my fee. It's already been agreed upon and the full amount paid up front. If you give me your bank account number, I'll...'

'No, don't bother,' Rafe broke in, not caring about the money this once. Les might need it. He wouldn't be running around covering too many weddings with a broken leg. 'You can owe me one. Just don't ask again, buddy. Not where a wedding is concerned. Must go. The doorbell's ringing. I'll call you back after the bride's gone. Let you know what I thought of her.'

Rafe hung up and headed downstairs, then hurried along towards the front door, curious now to see if Les was exaggerating about the bride-to-be's blonde beauty.

She'd have to be something really special to surprise him. After all, he was used to beautiful blondes. He'd photographed hundreds. He'd even fallen madly in love with one once.

He'd been twenty-five at the time, and had just started climbing the fashion photographic ladder. Liz had been an up-and-coming cat walk model. Nineteen, nubile and too nice to be true. Only he hadn't realised that in the beginning. He'd become so besotted with her he'd actually begged her to live with him. Which she had. But only till she'd milked him for everything he was worth, both personally and professionally. Within a year she'd moved on to an older, more influential photographer, leaving an emotionally bruised and embittered Rafe behind.

He was no longer bruised, or bitter. That had all happened years ago. But he hadn't lived with a girlfriend since, no matter how much he might occasionally be tempted to. And he didn't date blondes any more. Experience had taught him blondes often played sweet and vulnerable and not too bright, when they were actually smart as a whip, sneakily manipulative and ruthlessly ambitious.

Photographing them, however, was another question. A blonde was still his model of choice.

Rafe wrenched open the front door to his inner-city terrace home and tried not to stare. Wow! Les hadn't exaggerated one bit.

What a pity she was going to be married, he thought as his male gaze swept over his visitor. Because if ever there was a blonde who might make him reassess his decision never to date one again, she was standing right in front of him.

Talk about exquisite!

Ms Isabel Hunt was the epitome of an Alfred Hitchcock heroine. Classically beautiful and icily blonde, with cheekbones to die for, cool long-lashed blue eyes and what looked like a perfect figure. Though, to be honest, she would have to remove the fawn linen jacket she was wearing over those tailored black trousers for Rafe to be sure.

'Ms Hunt?' he said, smiling warmly at her. What had been an irksome task in his mind now held the prospect of some pleasure. Rafe liked nothing better than photographing truly beautiful women. Of course, only the camera would tell if she was also photogenic. It was perverse that some of the most beautiful women in the flesh didn't always come up so well on film.

'Mr Saint Vincent?' she returned, her own gaze raking over him. With not much approval, he noted. Maybe she didn't like men who hadn't shaved by noon.

She looked the fussy type. Her make-up was perfection and her clothes immaculate. That white shirt she had on underneath her jacket was so dazzlingly white, it could have featured in one of those washing-powder ads.

'The one and only,' he replied, his smile widening. Most women, he'd found, eventually responded to his smile. Rafe liked his photographic subjects to be totally relaxed with him. Being stiff in front of a camera was the kiss of death when it came to getting good results. 'But do call me Rafe.'

'Rafe,' she said obediently, but coolly.

Ms Hunt, Rafe realised ruefully, was not a woman given to being easily charmed. Which perhaps was just as well. She was one gorgeous woman. Those eyes. And that mouth! Perfectly shaped and deliciously full, her lips were provocative enough in repose. How would he react if they ever smiled at him?

Don't smile, lady, he warned her silently. Or we both could be in big trouble!

'Would you object if I called you Isabel?' he said recklessly.

'If you insist.'

Was that contempt he saw flicker in her eyes? Surely not!

Still, Rafe decided to pull right back on the charm for now and get down to tin tacks.

'Les rang me a little while ago with just the barest of details,' he informed her matter-of-factly, 'so why don't you come inside and we can discuss a few things?'

He led her into the front room where he conducted most of his business. It wasn't an office as such, more of a sitting room, simply and sparsely furnished. The walls, however, were covered with his favourite photos, all of women in various states of dress and undress. None actually nude, but some were close, and all were in black and white.

'I don't see any wedding photos,' the bride-to-be noted curtly as he led her over to the nearest sofa.

'I no longer work as a wedding photographer,' he admitted. 'But I was once Les's partner, so don't worry. I know what I'm doing.'

She gave him a long hard look. 'I suspect you're more expensive than Les.'

Rafe sat down on the navy sofa opposite hers and leant back, stretching his arms along the back.

'Usually,' he agreed. 'But not this time. I'm doing this job as a favour to Les.'

'What about the actual photos? Will I have to pay more for them?'

'No.'

She glanced up at the prints on the wall again and almost rolled her eyes. 'You do take coloured snaps, don't you?'

Rafe was not a man easy to rile. He had a very even temper. But she was beginning to annoy him. Coloured snaps, indeed! He wasn't some hack or hobby photographer. He was a professional!

'Of course,' he returned, priding himself on sounding a lot calmer than he was feeling inside. 'I do a lot of fashion photography. And fashion wouldn't be fashion without colour. But wedding photographs do look fab-

ulous in black and white. I think you'd be pleased with
the results.'

'Mr Saint Vincent—' she began frostily.

'Rafe, please,' he interrupted, determined not to lose
it. My, she was a snooty bitch. Mr Luke Freeman was
welcome to her. Rafe wondered if the poor groom knew
exactly what type he was getting here. Talk about an Ice
Princess!

'The thing is, *Rafe*,' she said in clipped tones, 'I
wouldn't have chosen a wine-red gown for my maid of
honour if I wanted all the photographs done in black and
white, would I?'

Rafe simply ignored her sarcasm. 'What colour is the
groom wearing?'

'Black.'

'And yourself?'

'White, of course.'

'Of course,' he repeated drily, his eyes holding hers
for much longer than was strictly polite.

She flushed. She actually flushed.

Rafe was startled. She *couldn't* be a virgin. Not at
thirty. And not looking like that. It was faintly possible,
he supposed. Either that, or sex wasn't her favourite pas-
time.

Rafe pitied the groom some more. It didn't look as if
his wedding night was going to be a ball if his bride
was this uptight about sex.

'I'm sorry but I really don't want my wedding photos
done in black and white,' she pronounced coldly, despite

her pink cheeks. 'If you feel you can't accommodate me on this, then I'll just have to find another photographer.'

'You won't find anyone decent at this late stage,' Rafe told her bluntly.

She looked frustrated and Rafe found some sympathy for her. He *was* being a bit stubborn, even if he *was* right.

'Look, Isabel, would you tell a painter how to paint? Or a surgeon how to operate? I'm a professional photographer. And a top one, even if I say so myself. I know what will look good, and you won't look just *good* shot in black and white. You'll look magnificent.'

She was clearly taken aback by his fulsome compliment. But he'd never had the opportunity to photograph a bride as beautiful as this. No way was he going to let her muck up his creative vision. With the automatic cameras now available, any fool could take colour snaps. But only Rafe Saint Vincent could produce black and white masterpieces!

'There will be any number of guests at your wedding taking coloured snaps, if you want some,' he argued. 'My job, however, is to give you quality photographic memories which will not only be beautiful, but timeless. I guarantee that you'll still be able to show your wedding photographs to your grandchildren with great pride. They won't be considered old-fashioned, or funny, in any way.'

'You're very sure of yourself, aren't you?' she threw at him in almost scornful tones.

'I'm very sure of my abilities. So what do you say?'

'I don't seem to have much choice.'

'You won't be disappointed if you hire me. Trust me on this, Isabel.'

She half rolled her eyes again.

Trust, Rafe realised, was something else Isabel Hunt did not do easily.

'Why don't you look at some of my more conventional black and white portraits?' he suggested, pushing over the album portfolio which lay on the coffee-table between them. 'You might find them reassuring. I confess the shots on my walls are somewhat...avant-garde. Meanwhile, I'm dying for a cup of coffee. I haven't been up all that long. Late night last night,' he added with a wry smile. 'Would you like one yourself? Or something else?'

'No, thank you. I've not long had breakfast.'

'Aah...late night, too?' he couldn't resist saying.

She looked right through him before dropping her beautiful but chilly blue eyes back to the album. She began flicking through it, insulting him with the little time she spent over each page.

He glowered down at the top of her head, and had to battle to control the crazy urge to bend over and wrench the pins out of her oh, so uptight French roll. His hands itched to yank her to her feet and shake her till her hair spilled down over her slender shoulders. He wanted to pull her to him and kiss her till there was fire in her eyes, not ice. He wanted to see that blush back in her cheeks. But not from embarrassment. From passion.

He wanted... He wanted... He wanted *her*!

Rafe reeled with shock. To desire this woman was insane. And stupid. And masochistic.

First, she was going to be married in two weeks. Second, she was a blonde. Third, she didn't even like him!

Three strikes and you're out!

Now go get your coffee, dummy. And when you come back, focus on her simply as a fantastic photographic subject, and not the most challenging woman of the century.

CHAPTER TWO

ISABEL did not look up till she was sure she was alone, shutting the photo album with a snap.

The man was impossible! To hire him as her wedding photographer was impossible! Rafe Saint Vincent might be a brilliant photographer but if he wasn't capable of listening to what *she* wanted, then he could just go jump.

Truly, men like him irritated the death out of her.

And attracted the devil out of her.

Isabel sighed. That was the main problem with him, wasn't it? The fact she found him wickedly sexy.

Isabel closed her eyes and slumped back against the sofa. She'd thought she'd finally cured herself of the futile flaw of fancying men like him. She'd thought since meeting and becoming engaged to Luke that she would never again need what such men had to offer.

Luke was exactly what she'd been looking for in a husband. He was handsome. Successful. Intelligent. And extremely nice. A man who, like her, had come to the conclusion that romantic love was not a sound basis for marriage, that compatibility and common goals were far more reliable. Falling in love, they'd both discovered in the past, made fools of men—and women. Passion might be the stuff poems were written about, but it didn't make you happy in the long run. Mind-blowing sex, Isabel now believed, was not the be-all and end-all when it came to a relationship.

Not that Luke wasn't good in bed. He was. If her mind sometimes strayed to her own private and personal fantasies while he was making love to her, and vice versa, then Isabel hadn't been overly concerned.

Till this moment.

It was one thing to fill her mind with images of some mythical stranger during sex with Luke. Quite another to go to bed with him on her wedding night thinking of the likes of Rafe Saint Vincent.

And she would, if he was around all that day, looking her up and down with those sexy eyes of his.

Isabel shook her head with frustration. She'd always been attracted to the Mr Wrongs of this world. The daredevils and the thrill-seekers. The charmers and the slick, smooth-tongued womanisers who oozed the sort of confidence she found a major turn-on.

Of course, she hadn't known they were Mr Wrongs to begin with. She'd thought they were interesting, exciting men. It had taken several wretched endings—especially the disaster with Hal—to force her to face the fact that her silly heart had no judgement when it came to the opposite sex. It picked losers and liars.

By her late twenties, desperation and despair had forced Isabel's brain to develop a fail-safe warning system. If she was madly attracted to a man, then that was a guarantee he was another Mr Wrong.

So she didn't have to know much about Rafe Saint Vincent to know his character. She only had to take one look at him. Les *had* provided her with some brief details about him—namely that he was a bachelor, and a brilliant photographer—but to be honest, aside from the warning bells going off in Isabel's brain, Mr Saint Vincent's appearance said it all, from his trendy black clothes to his earring and his designer stubble. The fact he lived in a terraced house in Paddington completed the picture of a swinging male single of the new millennium whose priorities were career, pleasure and leisure, and who was never going to buy a cow when he could have cartons of milk for free. Rafe might not be a criminal or a con man, like Hal had been, but he would always be a waste of time for a woman who wanted marriage and children.

Actually, *every* man Isabel had ever fancied had been a waste of time in that regard. Which was why, when she'd found herself staring thirty in the face, still without the home and family of her own she'd always craved, Isabel had decided enough was enough, and set about finding herself a husband with her head, not her heart.

And she had.

Isabel knew she could be happy with Luke. Very happy.

But the last thing she needed around on her wedding day was someone like Rafe Saint Vincent.

Yet she needed a photographer. What excuse could she give her mother for not hiring him? The black and white business wouldn't wash. Her mother just *loved* black and white photographs, a hangover from the days when that was all there was. Her mother was not a young woman. In fact she was seventy, Isabel having been the product of a second honeymoon when Doris Hunt had turned forty.

No, there was nothing for it but to hire Rafe God's-gift-to-women Saint Vincent. Isabel supposed there was no real harm in fantasising about another man while your husband was making love to you, even on your wedding night. Luke would never know if she never told him.

And she wouldn't.

Actually, there were a lot of things about herself she'd never told Luke. And she didn't aim on starting now!

Her eyes opened and lifted to the photographs on the wall again and, this time, with their creator out of the room, Isabel let her gaze linger.

They really were incredibly erotic, his clever use of shadow highly suggestive. Although the subjects were obviously either naked or semi-naked, the lighting was such that most private parts were hidden from view. There was the occasional glimpse of the side of a breast, or the curve of a buttock, but not much more.

Tantalising was the word which came to mind. Isabel could have stared at them for hours. But the sound of footsteps coming down the stairs had her reefing her eyes away and searching for something to do. Anything!

Fishing her mobile phone out of her bag, she punched in her parents' number and was waiting impatiently for her mother to answer when her nemesis of the moment walked back into the room, sipping a steaming mug of coffee.

She pretended she wasn't ogling him, but her eyes

snuck several surreptitious glances as he walked over and sat down in the same spot he'd occupied before. He was gorgeous! Tall and lean, just as she liked them. Not traditionally handsome in the face, but attractive, and oh, so sexy.

'Yes?' her mother finally answered, sounding slightly breathless.

'Me, here, Mum.' No breathlessness on Isabel's part. She sounded wonderfully composed. Yet, inside, her heartbeat had quickened appreciably. Practice *did* make perfect!

'Oh, Isabel, I'm so glad you rang before we left for the club. I was thinking of you. So how did it go with Mr Saint Vincent?'

'Fine. He was fine.'

Isabel saw his dark eyes widen over the rim of his coffee-mug. Clearly, he'd been thinking she wasn't going to hire him.

'As good as Les?' her mother asked. Les had been hired by her parents before, for their recent golden wedding anniversary party.

'Better, I'd say.'

'That's a relief. I've waited a long time to see you married, love. I would like to have some decent photographs of the momentous event.'

Isabel's eyes flicked up to the two most provocative photos on the wall and a decidedly indecent thought popped into her mind. What would it be like to be photographed by him like *that*? To be totally naked before him? To have him arranging filmy curtains or sliding satin sheets over her nude body? To have to stand—or lie—perfectly still in some suggestive pose for ages whilst he shot reel after reel of film, those sexy eyes of his focused only on her?

Just the thought of it sent her heartbeat even higher.

Fortunately, Isabel was not a female whose inner feelings showed readily on her face. She could look at a man and be thinking the hottest thoughts and still look cool. Sometimes, even uninterested. Which perhaps was just as well, or she'd have spent half of her life in bed.

She didn't flirt easily. Neither was she capable of the sort of coy sugary behaviour some men seemed to find both a come-on and a turn-on. Most men found her slightly aloof, even snobbish. They often confused her ice-blonde looks and ladylike manner with being prudish and undersexed. Which perhaps explained why most of her lovers had been men who dared to do what a gentleman wouldn't, men who simply rode roughshod over her seeming uninterest and simply took what they wanted.

Isabel looked at the man sitting opposite her and wondered what kind of lover he'd be.

Not that you're ever going to find out, her conscience reminded her harshly.

'I have to go, Isabel,' her mother was saying. 'Your father and I were just having a bite to eat before we go down the club. When will you be home? Will you be eating with us tonight?'

Isabel had been living with her parents during the last few weeks leading up to the wedding. She'd quit her flat, plus her job as receptionist at the architectural firm where Luke worked, content to become a career wife and home maker after their marriage. She and Luke were going to try for a baby straight away.

'As far as I know,' she told her mother whilst she continued to watch the man opposite with unreadable eyes. 'Unless Luke comes back today and wants to go out somewhere. If he happens to ring, you could ask him. And tell him I'll be back home by one at the latest.'

'Will do. Bye, love.'

'Bye, Mum.'

She clicked off the phone then bent down to tap it against the album on the coffee-table. 'Very impressive,' she said, giving him one of her super cool looks, the ones she fell back on when her thoughts were at their most shocking. Pity she couldn't have rustled one up earlier when his barb about her wearing white at her wedding had sent a most uncharacteristic flush to her cheeks. Still, she was back in control now. Thank heavens.

She put down the phone and opened the album to a page which held a traditional full-length portrait of a woman in an evening gown. 'I liked this portrait very much. If you feel you could reproduce shots like this, then you're hired.'

'I don't ever *reproduce* anything, Isabel,' he returned quite huffily. 'I'm an artist, not a copier.'

Isabel's patience began to wear thin. 'Do you want this job or not?' she threw at him.

'As I said before, I'm doing this as a favour to Les. The question is…do *you* want *me* or not?'

Isabel's eyes met his and she had a struggle to maintain her equilibrium. If only he knew…

'I suppose you'll have to do,' she managed to say.

'Such enthusiasm. When and where?'

How about here and now?

'The wedding is at four o'clock at St Christopher's Church at Burwood, a fortnight from today. And the reception is at a place in Strathfield called Babylon.'

'Sounds exotic.'

It was, actually. Isabel had a secret penchant for the exotic. Though you'd never tell by looking at her. She always dressed very conservatively. But her favourite story as a child had been Aladdin, and she'd often dreamt of being a harem girl, complete with sexy costume and gauzy veils over her face.

'Do you want me to come to your house beforehand?' he asked. 'A lot of brides want that. Though some are too nervous to pose well at that stage. Still, when I was doing weddings regularly, I developed a strategy for relaxing them which helped on some occasions.'

'Oh?' Isabel tried to stop her wicked imagination from taking flight once more, but it was a lost cause.

'I'd give them a good…stiff…drink,' he said between sips of his coffee.

How she kept a straight face, Isabel would never know.

'I don't drink,' she lied.

'Figures,' he muttered, and she almost laughed.

He obviously thought she was a prude.

'Don't worry,' she went on briskly. 'I won't be nervous. And, yes, I'm sure my mother will want you to come to the house beforehand. I'll jot down the address and phone number for you.' She pulled out a pen from her bag, plus a spare business card from her hairdresser, and wrote her parents' details on the back.

'What say you arrive on the day at two?' she suggested as she handed it over to him, then stood up.

He put down his coffee, stared at the card, then stood up also.

'Is this your regular hairdresser?' he asked.

The question startled her. 'Yes, why?'

'Did they do your hair today?'

'No. I did it myself. I only go to a hairdresser when I want a cut. I like to do it myself.' Aside from the money it cost, she wasn't fond of the way some hairdressers had difficulty following instructions.

'So you'll be doing your hair on your wedding day?'

'Yes.'

'Not like that, I hope,' he said as he slipped the card into his shirt pocket.

Isabel bristled. 'What's wrong with it like this?'

'It's far too severe. If you're going to have it up, you need something a little softer, with some pieces hanging around your face. Here. Like this.'

Before she could step away, or object, he was by her side, his fingers tugging at her hair and touching her cheeks, her ears, her neck.

It was one thing to keep her cool whilst she was just

thinking about him, quite another with his hands on her. His fingertips were like brands on her skin, leaving heated imprints in her flesh and sending quivery ripples down her spine.

'Your hair seems quite straight,' he was saying as he stroked several strands down in front her ears. 'Do you have a curling wand?'

'No,' she choked out, knowing she should step back from him but totally unable to. She kept staring at the V of bare skin in his open-necked shirt and wondering what he would look like, naked.

'I suggest you buy one, then. They're cheap enough.'

Her eyes lifted to find he was studying not her hair so much, but her mouth. For one long, horribly exciting moment, Isabel thought he was going to kiss her. She sucked in sharply, her lips falling apart as a shot of excitement zinged through her veins. But he didn't kiss her, and she realised with a degree of self-disgust that she'd just been hoping he would.

But what if he had? came the appalling thought. What if he *had*?

Just the *thought* of risking or ruining what she had with Luke made her feel sick.

'I must go,' she said, and bent to pick up her bag, the action forcing his hands to drop away from her face. By the time she'd straightened he'd stepped back a little. But she had to get out of there. And quickly.

'If I don't hear from you,' she added brusquely, 'then I will expect you to show up at my parents' home at two precisely, a fortnight from today. Please don't be late.'

'I am never late for appointments,' he returned.

'Good. Till then, then?'

He nodded and she swept past him, her bag brushing against him as she did so. She didn't apologise, or look down. She kept going, not drawing breath till she was in her car and on the road home.

Relief was her first emotion once his place was well out of sight. Then anger. At herself; at the Rafe Saint Vincents of this world; and at fate. Why couldn't Les have recommended a photographer like himself, a happily married middle-aged conservative bloke with three kids and a paunch?

When a glance in the rear-vision mirror reminded her she had bits of hair all over the place, courtesy of her Lord and Master, she pulled over to the kerb and pulled the pins out of her French roll, shaking her head till her hair fell down around her face like a curtain.

'Maybe you'd like me to wear it like this!' she stormed as she accelerated away again. 'Lucky for me it isn't longer, or you'd be suggesting I do a Lady Godiva act at my wedding. I could be the first bride ever to be photographed in the nude!'

She ranted and raved about him for a while, then at the traffic when it took her nearly twice as long to get home as it had to drive into the city. She was feeling more than a little stressed by the time she turned into her parents' street, her agitation temporarily giving way to surprise when she spotted Luke's blue car parked outside the house. She slid her navy car in behind it, frowning at Luke who was still sitting behind the wheel. When she climbed out, so did he, throwing her an odd look at her hair as he did so.

She felt herself colouring with guilt, which really annoyed her. She'd done nothing to be guilty about.

'Luke!' she exclaimed, trying not to sound as flustered as she was feeling. 'What on earth are you doing here? I wasn't expecting you. Why didn't you call me?'

'I tried your mobile phone a while back,' he said. 'But you didn't answer.'

'What? Oh, I must have left the blasted thing behind at the studio. I took it out to ring Mum and tell her how long I'd be.'

Isabel wanted to scream. How could she have been so stupid as to leave it behind? Now she'd have to go back for it. And she'd have to see that man again, *before* the wedding.

'Oh, too bad,' she muttered, slamming the car door. 'It can stay there till tomorrow. I'm not going back now.'

She could feel Luke's puzzled eyes on her and knew she wasn't acting like her usual calm self. She shook her head and threw him a pained look. 'You've no idea the dreadful day I've had. The photographer I booked for the wedding's had an accident and he made an appointment for me to meet this other man who's not really suitable at all. Brilliant, but one of those avant-garde types who wants to do everything in black and white. I pointed out that I wouldn't have selected a wine-red gown for my maid of honour if I'd wanted all the shots done in black and white, but would he listen to me? No! He even told me how he wanted me to wear my hair. As if I don't know what suits me best. I've never met such an insufferably opinionated man.'

Isabel knew she was babbling but she couldn't seem to stop.

'Still, what can you expect from someone who fancies himself an *artiste*. You know the type. Struts around like he's God's gift to women. And he wears this earring in the shape of a phantom's head, of all things. What a show pony! Goodness knows what our photographs are going to turn out like, but it's simply too late to get someone else decent. His name's Rafe—did I tell you? Rafe Saint Vincent. It wouldn't be his real name, of course. Just a career move. Nobody is born with a name like Rafe Saint Vincent. Talk about pretentious!'

Isabel finally ran out of steam, only to realise that Luke was not only staring at her as if she'd lost her mind, but that he wasn't looking his usual self, either.

Always well-groomed, Luke was the sort of man who kept 'tall, dark and handsome' at number one on every woman's most wanted list.

'Luke!' she exclaimed. 'You look like you've slept in your clothes. And you haven't even shaved. That's not like you at all.' Unlike other men she would not mention. 'What are you doing here, anyway? I thought you were going to stay in your father's old fishing cabin up on Lake Macquarie for the whole weekend.' And do some proper grieving, Isabel had hoped. The poor darling had to have been through hell this past fortnight since his parents' tragic deaths. Yet he'd been so brave about it all. And so strong.

'The cabin wasn't there any more,' he said. 'It had been torn down a few years before.'

'Oh, what a shame,' she murmured. But it explained why he was looking so disconsolate. 'So where did you stay last night? In a motel? Or a tent?' she added, hoping to jolly him up with a dab of humour.

'No.' He didn't crack even the smallest of smiles. 'Dad had built a brand-new weekender on the same site. I stayed there.'

'But...' Isabel frowned. 'How did you get in? You didn't break in, did you?'

'No. There was a girl staying there for the weekend and she let me in.'

Isabel was taken aback. 'And she let you *sleep* the night?'

Luke sighed. 'It's a long story, Isabel. I think we'd better go inside and sit down while I tell it to you.'

She tried not to panic. 'Luke, you're worrying me.'

When he took her arm and propelled her over to the front gate, she pulled out of his grip and lanced him with alarmed eyes. 'You're not going ahead with the wedding, are you?'

Isabel waited in an agony of anxiety for him to speak.

'No,' he finally answered, his expression grim. 'No, I'm not.'

CHAPTER THREE

ISABEL stared at him, aghast. 'Oh, no. No, Luke, don't do this to me!' Bursting into tears, she buried her stricken face in her hands.

'I'm so sorry, Isabel,' Luke said softly as he tried to take her into his arms.

'But why?' she wailed, gripping the lapels of his suit jacket and shaking them.

His eyes held apology. 'I've fallen in love.'

'Fallen in love!' she gasped. 'In less than a *day*?'

'No one is more surprised than me, I can tell you. But it's true. I came back straight away to tell you, and to call our wedding off.'

'But love's no guarantee of happiness, Luke,' she argued in desperation. 'I thought we agreed on that. It traps and tricks you. It really is blind. This girl you've supposedly fallen in love with—how do you know she'll be good for you? How do you know she won't make you miserable? You can't possibly know her real character, not this quickly. She could be playing a part for you, pretending to be something she's not. She might be a really bad person. A gold-digger, perhaps. A…a criminal even!'

'She's not *any* of those things,' he returned, looking

shocked by her arguments. 'She's a good person. I just know it.'

Isabel shook her head. One *day*! One miserable *day*! How could he know anything for sure? 'I would never have believed you could be so naïve,' she pronounced angrily. 'A man like you!'

'I'm not naïve,' he denied. 'Which is why I'm not rushing into anything. But I can't marry you, Isabel, feeling as I do about Celia. Surely you can see that.'

Isabel was not in the mood to see anything of the kind. She wanted to cry some more. And to scream. She'd been so close to having her dream come true. So darned close!

'Maybe I do and maybe I don't,' she grumbled, letting his lapels go. '*I'd* still marry *you*. I haven't much time for the highly overrated state of being in love.'

And she'd thought he felt the same way.

'Maybe that's because you've never really been in love,' Luke said.

Isabel's laugh was tinged with bitterness. 'I'm an expert in the subject. But that's all right. You'll live and learn, Luke Freeman, and when you do, give me a call. Meanwhile, let's go inside, as you said. I need a drink. Not tea or coffee. Something much stronger. Dad still has some of the malt whisky I gave him for his birthday. That should do the trick.'

Isabel let herself into the house, Luke following.

'But you don't drink Scotch,' he pointed out with a frown in his voice.

'Aah, but I do,' she threw over her shoulder at him

as she strode into her parents' lounge room, heading straight for the drinks cabinet in the corner. 'When the occasion calls for it,' she added, pouring herself half a glassful. 'Which is now. Today. This very second.'

She knocked back half of it, steadfastly refusing to shudder like some simpering female fool while it burnt a red-hot path down her throat. 'Ahh,' she said with a lip-smacking sigh of satisfaction once it reached its destination. 'That hits the spot. You want one?' she asked Luke, but he shook his head.

Swirling the amber liquid in her glass, she walked over and settled in one of her mother's large comfy armchairs, her feet curled up under her. Hooking her hair behind her ear with her left hand, she lifted the whisky to her lips and took another deep swallow. She glanced over at Luke, who was still standing near the doorway, looking startled by her behaviour.

Isabel supposed she wasn't living up to the image he obviously had of her. Up till today it had been easy to play the role of the super-serene, super-sensible fiancée who was never fazed or upset by anything he did. Because he'd never done anything to really upset her.

Clearly, he didn't know what to make of her as her real self, instead of Lady Isabel, the unflappable.

But did he honestly think he could roll up and tell her their wedding was off at this late stage with no trouble at all? Did he imagine she wouldn't be hurt by his obviously being unfaithful to her last night?

The realisation that she had been mentally unfaithful to *him* today tempered her inner fury somewhat, and brought some sympathy and understanding for Luke's actions. Marriages made with the head and not the heart might have worked in the past, she appreciated. But in this modern day and age, with all the abounding sexual temptations, such a union was a disaster waiting to happen.

Still, she would be surprised if it was true love compelling Luke to do this. More likely that good deceiver *lust*!

'I suppose she's beautiful, this Celia,' she said drily.

'I think so.' Luke finally sat down as well.

'What does she do?'

'She's a physiotherapist.'

A physiotherapist. Not only beautiful but clever and educated as well.

Isabel hadn't embraced tertiary studies after leaving high school. Her exam results hadn't been good enough. Oh, she wasn't dumb, just not focused on her school work. She'd been far too interested in boys at the time, much to her parents' dismay.

She had managed a brief receptionist course at tech. That, combined with her looks, had meant she'd been rarely out of a job. Over the years she'd become a top receptionist, computer literate and very competent.

Yet she'd never really been interested in a career as such. She'd always wanted marriage and motherhood. It irked Isabel that this Celia, however innocently, had stolen the one man who might have given her both.

'And what was she doing, staying in your father's weekender? Did he rent it out?'

'No. She's his mistress's daughter.'

'His *what*?' Isabel's feet shot out from under her as she snapped forward on the chair.

'Dad's mistress's daughter,' Luke repeated drily.

Isabel gaped. 'No! I don't believe you. Not *your* dad. With a *mistress*? That's impossible. He was one of the best husbands and fathers I've ever met. He was one of the reasons I wanted to marry you. Because I believed you'd be just as good a family man.'

'As I said…it's a long story.'

'And a fascinating one, I'm sure,' Isabel mused. 'It seems the Freeman men have a dark side I don't know about.'

'Could be,' Luke agreed ruefully.

'I wish I'd known about it sooner,' she muttered, and swigged back the last of the whisky in her glass.

Luke shot her a puzzled look. 'What do you mean by that?'

'Oh, nothing. Just a private joke. I have this perverse sense of humour sometimes. Come on, tell me all the naughty details.'

'I hope you won't be too shocked.'

She chuckled. 'Oh, dear, that's funny. Me, shocked? Trust me, darling. I can never be seriously shocked by anything sexual.'

Luke frowned at her. 'Did I ever really know you, Isabel?'

'Did I ever really know *you*?' she countered saucily.

Their eyes met and they smiled together.

'You'll find someone else, Isabel,' Luke said with total confidence.

'I dare say I will. But not quite like you, darling. You were one in a million. Your Celia is one lucky girl. I hope you'll be very happy together.' Privately, she didn't think they would be, but who knew? Maybe Luke was a better picker than herself when it came to falling in love. *If* he was really in love, that was.

'Thanks, Isabel. That's very generous of you. But we won't be rushing to the altar. Which reminds me. I will, of course, be footing the bill for any expenses your parents have encountered with the wedding. I'll send them a cheque which should cover everything, and with some left over. And I'll be doing the right thing by you, too.'

She shook her head, then slipped the solitaire-diamond engagement ring off her finger. 'No, Luke. I wasn't marrying you for your money. I know you might have thought I was, but I wasn't. I was just pleased you were successful and stable. I wanted that security for my children. And for myself.'

When she went to give him the ring, he refused to take it. 'I don't want that ring back, Isabel. It's yours. I gave it to you. You keep it, or sell it if you want to.'

Isabel came close to crying again. He really was the nicest man. He'd have made a wonderful father.

She shrugged and slipped the ring onto her right hand. 'If you insist,' she said, using every bit of her will-power to keep it together. 'But I won't sell it. I'll wear it. It's a beautiful ring. Fortunate, though, that I didn't find any wedding rings I liked yesterday, so at least we don't have to return *them*.'

Isabel was still amazed by the fact that less than twenty-four hours ago Luke had been very happy with her. But, as they said in the classics, there was many a slip 'twixt the cup and the lip.

She sighed, then stared regretfully into her now empty glass. 'I'd better go get you your credit card while you're here.' And while she could still stand. That whisky was *really* working now.

'That can wait,' Luke said before she could get up. 'I want to finish discussing the rest of my financial obligations first.'

She frowned. 'What other financial obligations could you possibly have?'

'I owe you, Isabel. More than a ring's worth.'

'No, you don't, Luke. I never lived with you. I have no claim on you other than the expenses for the wedding.'

'That's not the way I see it. You gave up your job to become my wife. You expected to be going on your honeymoon in a fortnight's time and possibly becoming a mother in the near future. Aside from that, married to me, you would never have had to worry about money for the rest of your life. I can't help you with the honeymoon or the becoming a mother bit now, but I can give you the financial security for life that you deserve.'

'Luke, truly, you don't have to do this.'

'Yes. I do. Now listen up.'

Isabel listened up, amazed when Luke insisted she

have his town house in Turramurra, as well as a portfolio of blue-chip stocks and shares which would provide her with an independent income for life. It seemed his father had been a very rich man. And now so was Luke.

She thought about refusing, but then decided that would just be her pride talking. At least now she wouldn't have to worry about having to live here under her parents' roof till she found another job. Her mother was going to be very upset when she found out the wedding was off.

She smiled a wry smile at this wonderful man she had hoped to marry. 'I always knew you were a winner. But I'd have preferred you as my husband rather than my sugar-daddy.'

'You've no idea how sorry I am about all this, Isabel,' Luke apologised again. 'I wouldn't have hurt you for the world. You're a great girl. But the moment I saw Celia, I was a goner.'

Isabel's mind flew straight to the moment she first saw Rafe Saint Vincent today. She hadn't been a goner. But she might have been, if he'd come on to her. Thank heaven he hadn't,

'She must be something, this Celia.'

'She's very special.'

And very beautiful, no doubt, Isabel deduced, with a body made for sin and eyes which drew you and held you and corrupted you. Just as Rafe's eyes had today.

He'd fancied her. Isabel hadn't liked to admit it to herself before this, but she'd sensed his male interest at the time. She'd sensed it from the first second they'd looked at each other. She always sensed things like that.

You could go back for your phone after Luke leaves. You could tell Rafe the wedding's off. You could...

No, no, she screamed at herself. Not again. Never again!

'Okay, so tell me all,' she demanded of Luke, desperately needing distraction from her escalatingly dangerous thoughts. 'And don't leave out anything...'

CHAPTER FOUR

RAFE noticed the phone she'd left behind almost immediately. He snatched it up from the coffee-table and was running out after her when he stopped and waited to see if she remembered and came back for it herself.

But she didn't, and he just stood in the hallway and listened to her drive off.

It was crazy to want to see her again this side of the wedding. Crazy to force her to return.

She wasn't the type to let him have his wicked way with her. She wasn't the type to let *any* man have his wicked way with her without a band of gold on her finger.

Maybe not a virgin, but close. The way she'd frozen when he'd dared touch her hair. The way she'd bolted out of his place, probably in fear that he might do more.

And he'd wanted to. Oh, yes. Being that close to her—actually touching her—had turned him on something rotten. When her bag had hit him as she'd hurried out, he'd just managed not to visibly wince. Luckily, she hadn't stopped and looked down at where her bag had hit him, or she'd have been in for one big fright!

That was another reason why he hadn't run out into the street after her just now. Looking a fool was not his favourite occupation.

Hopefully, by the time Isabel realised she'd left her phone and turned round to come back, he'd have himself under control again.

And then what, Rafe? What is the point of this exercise? Is it some form of sexual masochism?

Even if you were the kind of man who seduced other men's fiancées—which you're not, usually—you haven't one chance in Hades of defrosting *this* one.

So, if and when she does come back, have the damned phone handy near the front door, give it to the lady and send her on her merry way.

His decision made, Rafe dropped the metallic-blue cellphone on the hall table and headed upstairs for some breakfast. After that, he came back downstairs to his darkroom, where he set about developing the rolls of film he'd shot last night at Orsini's summer fashion parade, and at the after-parade party, which had gone well into the wee small hours of the morning. The women's magazines would be ringing first thing Monday morning, wanting to see the best of them.

Two hours later, Rafe was still in his darkroom, going through the motions, but his mind simply wasn't on the job. The object of his distraction hadn't come back, and he simply could not put her out of his head.

The truth was, she intrigued him. Not just sexually, but as a person. He wanted to know more about her.

In the end, Rafe stopped trying to put her out his mind. He abandoned his work, pulled the business card she'd left him out of his pocket, went back upstairs, picked up his phone and punched in the number she'd written down.

The line rang and rang at the other end, with Rafe about to hang up when someone finally picked up.

'Hello there.'

Rafe frowned. It was a woman, but he wasn't sure if it was Isabel. She sounded…odd. 'Isabel?'

'Yep? To whom do I have the pleasure of speaking?'

Rafe couldn't believe his ears. She was drunk!

'It's Rafe. Rafe Saint Vincent. The photographer.'

Dead silence. Though he could hear her breathing.

'You left your mobile phone at my place.'

More silence.

'I thought you might be worried about it.'

She actually laughed.

'Isabel,' he said with concern in his voice. 'Have you been drinking?'

'Mmm. You might say that.'

'I am saying it.'

'So what?'

Rafe was taken aback. This wasn't the woman he'd met today. This was someone else. 'You said you didn't drink,' he reminded her.

She laughed again. 'I lied.'

His eyes widened with shock, then narrowed with worry. 'Isabel, what's wrong? What's happened?'

'I guess there's no point in not telling you. You'll have to know some time, anyway. The wedding's off.'

He couldn't have been more taken aback, both by the news *and* her manner. 'Why?' he asked.

'Luke's left me for someone else.'

Rafe experienced a small secret thrill at this news, but his overriding emotion was sympathy. He knew what it was like to be left for someone else, and he wouldn't wish the experience on a dog.

'I'm so sorry, Isabel,' he said with genuine feeling. 'You must be feeling rotten.'

'I was, till I downed my third whisky. Now, I actually don't feel too bad.'

He had to smile. That was exactly what he'd done the day Liz had left him. Hit the bottle. 'You should never drink alone, you know,' he warned softly.

'Oh, I'm not drunk,' she denied, even though her voice was slurring a little. 'Just tipsy enough so that my pain is pleasantly anaesthetised. Why, you offering to drink with me, lover?'

Rafe's smile widened. It seemed Isabel's ice-princess act melted considerably under the influence of three glasses of Scotch.

'I think you've had enough for one day.'

'That's not for you to say,' she huffed.

'Maybe not, but I'm still saying it.'

'Did anyone ever tell you that you are the bossiest person alive?'

'Yeah. My mother. She threw a party the day I left home.'

'I can well imagine.'

'But she loves me all the same.'

'I doubt other people would be so generous.'

Her alcohol-induced sarcasm amused him. 'Did any-one ever tell you you're a snooty bitch?' he countered.

He liked it when she laughed. Being drunk suited her. No more Miss Prissy. How he wished he was with her now.

There again, perhaps it was wise that he wasn't. When and if he took her to bed, he didn't want her drunk. Or on the rebound. He wanted her wanting him for himself, and no other reason.

'I guess you won't be needing my services now,' he said.

'As a photographer, you mean?'

Rafe sucked in sharply. What a provocative reply! Perhaps she didn't disapprove of him as much as he'd thought she had.

Or perhaps it was just the drink talking.

'Actually, I'd still like to photograph you,' he said, truthfully enough.

'Really? Why?'

'Why? Well, firstly, you are one seriously beautiful woman, and I have a penchant for photographing beauti-ful women. Secondly, I just want to see you again. I want to take you out to dinner somewhere.'

'You mean…like…on a date?'

'Yes. Exactly like that.'

'You don't waste much time, do you? I've only been dumped for two hours. And you've only known about it for two minutes! What if I said I was too broken up over Luke to date anyone for a while?'

'Then I'd respect that. But I'd ask you out again next week. And the week after that.'

'I should have guessed you'd be the determined type,' she muttered.

'Being determined is not a vice, Isabel.'

'That depends. So why is it you don't already have a girlfriend? Or *do* you? Don't lie to me, now. I hate men who lie to me,' she added, slurring her words.

'I'm between girlfriends at the moment.'

'Oh? What happened to the last one?'

'She went overseas to work. I wasn't inclined to follow her.'

'Why?'

'My career is here, in Australia.'

'Ahh. Priority number one.'

'What does that mean?'

'It means no, thank you very much, Rafe. I've been down that road far too many times to travel it again.'

'Now I'm confused. What road are you referring to?'

'Dating men who want only one thing from me. You do only want one thing from me, don't you, Rafe?'

Rafe considered that a loaded question.

'I wouldn't say that, exactly.' He liked talking to her, too. 'But I have to confess that marriage and kiddies are not on my list of must-do things in my life.'

'Well, they're on mine, Rafe. And sooner, rather than later. But I appreciate your telling me the truth. That's a big improvement on some of the other men I've become involved with in the past.'

His eyebrows shot up. It sounded as if there had been

scads. Any idea that she might almost be a virgin went out of the window. It just showed you first impressions weren't always right.

'Did your fiancé lie to you?'

'Luke? Oh, no…no, Luke was no liar.'

'But he was obviously two-timing you,' he pointed out.

'No. He wasn't. Look, it's rather difficult to explain.'

'Try.'

So she did, explaining the circumstances which had led up to Luke's meeting Celia.

'So he hasn't been two-timing me,' she finished up. 'He only met Celia yesterday.'

'Perhaps, but he didn't tell you the truth about why he was going up to his dad's fishing cabin on Lake Macquarie in the first place, did he?'

'No, but I can understand why. He'd been thrown for a loop when the solicitor told him his Dad wanted to leave his weekender to some strange woman.'

'You make a lot of excuses for him, don't you? He was still unfaithful to you. And he hurt you, Isabel.'

'He didn't mean to. Look, I'm sorry I told you about it now. It's really none of your business. Thank you for ringing and for making me feel a little better, but I think we should leave it right there, don't you? As I said, we want different things in life. I wonder…could you possibly post my phone back to me?'

'I'd rather drop it off to you.'

'And I'd rather you didn't.'

'You're afraid of me,' he said, startled by this realisation.

'Don't be ridiculous!'

Oh-oh. She was definitely sobering up. And returning to her former stroppy self.

'Just tell me one thing.'

'What?'

'Did you love him?'

'I was marrying him,' she snapped. 'What do *you* think?'

'I think that's a very evasive answer. For a person who demands the truth from others, you're not too good at delivering it yourself.'

She sighed. 'Very well. I liked and respected Luke, but, no, I did not love him. Satisfied?'

'Not even remotely,' Rafe said ruefully. 'Did you think *he* loved *you*?'

'No.'

'What on earth kind of marriage was *that* going to be?'

'One that lasted.'

'Oh, yeah, right. It didn't even get through the engagement. For pity's sake, Isabel, what did you expect? Men want passion from their wives. And sex. At least in the beginning.'

'You think I didn't give Luke sex?'

'Not the kind which his new dolly-bird obviously does.'

'You don't know what you're talking about. Look, I'm sorry I started this conversation. You simply don't have the capacity to understand what Luke and I had together. How could you? You're one of those men who lives for himself and himself alone. A woman is just a passing pleasure to you, a bit of R&R from your work. You don't want a real relationship with one. As for children, you probably see them as inconveniences, little ankle-biters who'd get in the way of your lifestyle. Luke wasn't like that. He wanted a family. Like me. He wanted for ever. Like me. We might not have been madly in love but we were good friends and extremely compatible, *in* bed as well as out. We could have had a happy marriage. I don't believe he's in love with this new dolly-bird, as you call her. He only met her yesterday. I think it's just sex, the kind that obsesses you so much sometimes that you can't think straight.'

Rafe's eyes widened. It sounded as if she'd been there, done that. She was becoming more interesting by the minute.

'That kind of physical affair never lasts,' she finished bitterly.

Yep. She'd been there, done that, all right. Rafe didn't know if he felt tantalised by this knowledge, or jealous. Either way, the thought of Isabel in the throes of an all-consuming sexual passion was an intriguing one.

'Is that what you're hoping?' he suggested. 'That maybe this thing your Luke is having with this girl won't last? That maybe he'll wake up on Monday morning, realise he's made a big mistake and beg you to take him back?'

'Well, actually, no. I hadn't been hoping that. But now that you've mentioned the possibility…'

Luke could have kicked himself.

'Don't start grasping at straws, Isabel.'

'I'm not. But I'm also not going to repeat the mistakes of my past. So, thank you for thinking of me, Rafe. But find someone else to photograph, and to take to dinner, because it isn't going to be me.'

'Isabel, please…'

'No, Rafe,' she said sternly. 'I realise you have difficulty in accepting that word, but it's definitely no. Now I must go. Goodbye.'

And she hung up on him.

Swearing, Rafe slammed down his end of the phone. He'd handled that all wrong. Totally abysmally wrong!

Still, perhaps it *was* for the best. Isabel wanted marriage. Whereas he most definitely didn't.

But she was wrong about what he wanted from her. It wasn't just sex.

Oh, come now, the voice of brutal honesty piped up. It's always just sex you're looking for these days. All that other stuff you offer a female is nothing but foreplay. The chit-chat. The photographing. The dinner dates. All with one end in view. Getting whatever pretty woman has taken your eye into bed and keeping her there on and off till you grow bored.

Which you always do in the end. Admit it, man, you've become shallow and selfish with women, exactly as Isabel said you were. You haven't been worth two bob since Liz left you. She stuffed you, buddy. Took away your heart. Isabel was right not to get involved with you. You're a dead loss to someone like her. Go back to work. That's the only thing you're good for. Creating images. Anything real is just too much for you.

He stomped downstairs, still muttering. Till he saw Isabel's shiny blue cellphone on the hall table. How odd that just seeing something she owned gave him a thrill.

Did he dare still take it back to her?

No, he decided. She'd said no. He had to respect that. He'd post it to her on Monday, as she'd asked.

Feeling more empty and wretched than he had in years, Rafe returned to his darkroom and tried to bury himself in the one thing which had always sustained him, even in his darkest moments.

But, for the second time that day, his precious craft failed to deliver the distraction he craved.

CHAPTER FIVE

ISABEL groaned. She'd handled that all wrong; talked too much; revealed too much.

Alcohol always made her talkative.

She thanked her stars that she'd pulled herself together towards the end—and that she'd had enough courage to resist temptation.

But oh, she'd wanted to say yes. To everything he'd offered. The photography. The dinner date. Sex afterwards, no doubt.

Isabel closed her eyes at the thought.

They sprang open again at another thought. Her mobile!

Would he still post it to her after all she'd said to him? Her assassination of his character had been a bit brutal, even if correct. He hadn't denied a single word. Okay, so the man did have a sweet side. But how much of that was real? Maybe he'd just learnt that you caught more with honey than with salt.

If he was really sweet, then he'd post her phone back. If not?

Isabel shrugged. She couldn't worry about a phone. If she never got it back, then she'd report it lost and get another one. After all, she didn't have to watch her pennies any more. She was an independently wealthy woman now. Or she would be soon.

Luke would be as good as his word. That, she knew.

Isabel wandered down the hallway to her mother's kitchen, thinking about Luke. Was it possible he might change his mind about this Celia? Or was she simply looking for an excuse not to tell her parents the wedding was off when they came home?

Just the thought of their reaction—especially her mother's—made Isabel shudder. If she hadn't been over the drink-driving limit, she'd pack up her car right now and make a bolt for the town house Luke had given her. She had her own set of keys.

Unfortunately, as it was, there was nothing but to stay here and face the music.

The music, as it turned out, was terrible. Her father recovered somewhat after Isabel explained Luke was going to recompense them for everything they'd spent. But her mother could not be so easily soothed, not even when Isabel told her what Luke was doing for *her* in a financial sense. When Isabel repeated Luke's suggestion that her parents go on their pre-booked holiday to Dream Island, her mother's face carried horror.

'You think I could be happy going on what should have been your honeymoon?' she exclaimed. 'No wonder Luke left you for another woman. You have no sensitivity at all! I dare say he worked out that you were only marrying him for his money. So he gave you what you wanted, then looked elsewhere for some genuine love and warmth.'

Isabel was stunned by her mother's harsh words. 'You think I was only marrying Luke for his money?'

Her mother flushed, but still looked her straight in the eye. 'You weren't in love with the man. *That*, I know. I've seen you in love, girl, and what you felt for Luke wasn't it. You cold-bloodedly set out to get that man. I didn't say a word because I thought Luke would make a fine husband and father, and I hoped that you might eventually fall in love with him. You played false with him, Isabel. And you got what you deserved.'

'Dot, stop it,' Isabel's father intervened sharply. 'What's done is done. And who knows? Maybe it's all for the best. Maybe someone better will come along, someone our girl can like *and* love.'

Isabel gave her father a grateful look. But she was close to tears. And very hurt by her mother's lack of sympathy and understanding. 'I…I have to go and ring Rachel,' she said, desperate to get away from her mother's hostility. Rachel would at least be on her side.

'What about everyone else?' her mother threw after her. 'Who's going to make all the other phone calls necessary to cancel everything?'

'I'll do all that, Mum.'

'On *our* phone?'

Isabel closed her eyes for a second. Phones. They were her nemesis today. 'No,' she said wearily. 'I'll be moving into the town house Luke gave me tomorrow. I'll make all the calls from there.'

'You're moving out?' Suddenly, her mother looked wretchedly unhappy.

Isabel sighed. 'I think I should.'

'You…you don't have to, you know,' her mother said, her voice and chin wobbling. 'I don't really care about the phone bill.'

Isabel understood then that her mother had been lashing out from her own hurt and disappointment. She'd always wanted to see her only daughter married. And now that event seemed highly unlikely.

Because her mother was right, Isabel conceded. She *had* set out to get Luke rather cold-bloodedly, and she simply couldn't do that again. Which left what? Falling in love with another Mr Wrong?

No! Now that was on *her* list of never-do-again.

'It's all right, Mum,' Isabel said, giving her mother a hug. 'Everything will be all right. You'll see.'

Her mother began to cry then, with Isabel struggling not to join in.

She looked beseechingly at her father over her Mum's dropped head and he nodded. 'Go ring Rachel,' he said quietly. 'I'll look after her.'

Rachel, who was Isabel's only real female friend and now the owner of an unused wine-red bridesmaid dress, answered on the first ring.

'Can you talk?' was Isabel's first question. 'Have I rung at a bad time?'

Rachel's life was devoted to minding her foster-mother who had Alzheimer's. She'd been doing it twenty-four hours a day, seven days a week, for over four years now. Despite being a labour of love, it was a grinding existence with little pleasure or leisure.

Rachel's decision to take on this onerous task after her foster-mum's husband had deserted her, had cost her her job as a top secretary at the Australian Broadcasting Corporation, and her own partner at the time. Sacrifice, it seemed, was not a virtue men aspired to.

Nowadays, Rachel made ends meet by doing clothes alterations at home. Her only entertainment was reading and watching television, plus one night out a month which Isabel paid for and organised. Last night had actually been one of those times, Isabel taking her friend to Star City Casino for dinner then a show afterwards. It was a pleasing thought that she'd have the time and the money to take Rachel out more often now.

'It's okay,' Rachel said. 'Lettie's asleep. Thank goodness. It's been a really bad day. She didn't even know me. Or she pretended not to. She's always difficult the day after I've been out with you. I don't think she likes anyone else but me minding her.'

'Poor Rachel. I'm sorry to ring you with more bad news.'

'Oh, no, what's happened?'

'The wedding's off.'

'The miserable bastard,' was Rachel's immediate response, which rather startled Isabel.

'What makes you think it was Luke's doing?'

'I know you, Isabel. No way would you opt out of marrying Luke. So what was it? Another woman?'

'How did you guess?' Isabel said ruefully.

'It wasn't hard. Men are so typical.'

'Mum blames me. She says Luke looked elsewhere because I didn't love him.'

'You *confessed* it wasn't a romantic match?'

'No, she guessed.'

'Oh, well, you have to agree she had a few clues to go on. Luke wasn't your usual type. Too traditionally good-looking and far too straight-down-the-line.'

'Mmm. It turned out he wasn't quite the Mr Goody-Two-Shoes I thought he was. Not once he met the sexy Celia.'

'So who is sexy Celia? Where and when did he meet her?'

'He only met her yesterday, and she's his father's mistress's daughter.'

'*What*?' Rachel choked out. 'Would you like to repeat that?'

She did, along with the rest of Luke's story. Isabel had to admit it made fascinating listening. It wasn't every day that a son found out his high-profile hero-status father had been cheating on his mother for twenty years. Or that the same engaged and rather strait-laced son would jump into bed with the mistress's daughter within an hour or two of meeting her.

Isabel still did not believe that Luke was in love with this Celia, but he obviously thought he was after spending all night with her doing who knew what. Even now he was speeding back up to his dad's secret love-nest on Lake Macquarie for more of the same!

It sounded like an episode from a soap opera.

No, a *week* of episodes!

Rachel's ear was glued to the phone for a good fifteen minutes.

'You didn't tell your mother all that, did you?' she asked at the end of it.

'No. I just said he'd met someone else, fallen in love with her and decided he couldn't go through with the wedding.'

'At least he was decent enough to do that. A lot of guys these days would have tried to have their cake and eat it too, a bit like Luke's father did with this Celia's poor mother for twenty years.'

'Yes. I thought of that. But I also wondered if Luke might eventually realise it wasn't love he felt for Celia, but just good old lust.'

'Could be. So you'd take him back if he changed his mind?'

'In a shot.'

'Maybe I shouldn't alter my bridesmaid dress just yet, then.'

'Maybe not.'

'And maybe you shouldn't cancel the reception place, or the cake, or the photographer. Not for a couple of days, anyway.'

Isabel wished Rachel hadn't mentioned the photographer. She didn't want to think about Rafe.

'Oh, dear, I think Lettie's just called out for me,' Rachel said. 'Amazing how she's remembered my name now that I'm on the phone. I must go, Isabel. And I am sorry. But...'

'Don't you dare tell me it's all for the best,' Isabel warned.

Rachel laughed. 'All right, I won't. Keep in touch.'

'I will.' When Isabel got off the phone, she realised she hadn't told Rachel about her financial windfall. But she would, the next time she rang her.

Meanwhile, she set about packing her clothes. She was emptying the drawers in her old dressing table when her mother came into the bedroom, looking miserable and chastened.

'I feel terrible about what I said to you earlier, Isabel. Your father said I should have my tongue cut out.'

'It's all right, Mum. You were upset.'

'What I said. I...I don't think you were marrying Luke just for his money. I know you liked him a lot, too.'

'Yes, I did.'

'Do...do you think he might not have fallen for this other girl if you'd slept with him before the wedding?'

Isabel turned to stare at her mother. Truly, what world did she live in? 'Mum,' she said with a degree of exasperation, 'I did sleep with him. Quite often.'

'Oh...'

'And he liked it. A lot.'

'Oh!'

'Sex wasn't the problem. It was passion.'

'Passion?'

'Yes, that overwhelming feeling you get when you look at a person and you just have to be with them.'

'Jump into bed, you mean?'

'Yes. Luke and I never really felt like that about each other.'

'I used to feel that way about your dad,' her mother whispered, 'when we were first married. And he felt that way about me, too.'

Isabel smiled at her. 'That's good, Mum. That's how it should be.'

'Maybe your dad's right. Maybe you'll find someone nicer than Luke, someone you'll fall deeply in love with and who'll feel the same way about you.'

'I hope so, Mum. I really do.' It would be cruel to take away her mother's hope. She'd always had this dream of seeing her daughter as a bride. Isabel had had the same dream.

But not any more.

'You're still going to move out?' her mother asked a bit tearily.

Isabel stopped what she was doing to face her mother. 'Mum, I'm thirty years old. I'm a grown woman. I have to make my own life away from home, regardless. I only moved back in for a while because it was sensible and convenient, leading up to the wedding.'

'But I...I've liked having you home. You are very good company.'

Isabel thought the compliment came just a bit late.

'You're a good cook, too. Your dad and I are going to miss the meals you've cooked for us.'

Isabel relented and gave her mother another hug. 'What say I come over and cook you a meal once in a while? Will that do?'

'Just so long as you come over. Don't be a stranger.'

'I won't. I promise.'

'And you've forgiven your old mum?'

Isabel smiled a wry smile. 'Have you forgiven me for not giving you some grandchildren by now?'

'Having children isn't everything, Isabel.'

Isabel gave her a dry look. 'Said by a woman who had five.'

'Then I should know. What you need to do is find the right man. Then the children will follow.'

'Don't you think I've been trying to do that?'

'Don't try so hard. You're a beautiful girl. Just let nature take its course.'

Isabel was tempted to tell her that nature always led her up the garden path into the arms of men who'd never give her children.

But it was too late to confess such matters. She'd never told her mother the bitter truth about her boyfriends. She hadn't wanted to shock her. To reveal all now would only make her look even worse than she already did in her mother's eyes.

'Are you sure you don't want to go on that Dream Island holiday, Mum?' she asked, deciding a change of subject was called for.

'Positive. I'm too old that for that kind of holiday, anyway. Look, why don't you go yourself?'

'It's not a place you go alone.'

'Then ask a friend to go with you.'

Isabel thought immediately of Rafe... He'd jump at the chance of going with her, all expenses paid!

It was a tantalising idea. Did she dare? Could she actually *do* something like that without getting emotionally involved?

Perhaps she could. Her experience with Luke had changed her, made her stronger and much more self-reliant. She'd gone after what she wanted for once, listening to her head and not her heart. She'd actually gone to bed with a man she didn't love, and quite enjoyed it. Her mind no longer irrevocably linked sexual pleasure and being in love.

Just because Rafe was more like the type of man she'd used to fall in love with willy-nilly, that didn't mean she would fall in love this time. She also had the added advantage of knowing in advance that he wasn't interested in marriage or children. There would never be any fooling herself that she had a future with him.

He'd just be a passing pleasure. A salve to her pride and a comfort to her bruised female ego. Not to mention a comfort to her female body!

By the time she got through the next fortnight, cancelling everything and putting up with everyone's condolences, she'd need comforting. And what better way than on a balmy tropical island in the arms of a gorgeous man you fancied like mad, and who seemed to fancy you in return?

'Isabel?'

Isabel shook herself out of her provocative thoughts. 'Yes, Mum?'

'Well, what do you think about finding a friend to go

away on that holiday with you? If you can't get your money back, it does seem a shame to waste it.'

'We'll see, Mum.' She'd better sleep on the idea. She'd been knocked for a couple of sixes today. And she *had* been drinking. The booked holiday on Dream Island didn't start for another fortnight and she doubted Rafe was going anywhere in a hurry. Maybe if she felt the same way in the cold light of Monday morning…

A shiver ran down Isabel's spine at the thought of doing something that bold. It was one thing to deliberately go to bed with a man like Luke, when your intention was marriage. Quite another to contemplate a strictly sexual affair with the likes of Rafe Saint Vincent!

CHAPTER SIX

RAFE didn't sleep well that night, which wasn't like him. Usually, he was out like a light soon after his head hit the pillow.

But not this time. He tossed and turned. Even got up on one occasion and poured himself a stiff drink.

The trouble with that, however, was it reminded him even more forcibly of the reason for his insomnia.

Had she drunk some more after hanging up on him? Was she also up, wandering around the house in her nightie with another glass of whisky clutched in her hands?

He carried that image of her back to bed with him and tossed and turned some more, his hormone-revved head wondering what kind of nightie it might be. Short or long? Provocative or prissy?

Various alternatives came to mind. She'd look delicious in long creamy satin, and wickedly sexy in short black lace. Better still in nothing at all.

His groan was the groan of a man suffering from a case of serious sexual frustration. Which would never do if he wanted to get some sleep. And he did. He hadn't finished his work today and he'd have to beaver away at it all day tomorrow. No Sunday brunch down at

Darling Harbour with his mother. No slouching around watching the cooking shows on satellite.

Dragging himself up again, he made his way into the bathroom, where he had the hottest of hot showers, a technique he'd found worked much better on him than cold. The heat sapped his energy, and relaxed his tense muscles and other aching parts. After a good twenty minutes of sauna-type soaking, he snapped off the water, dried himself with one of his extra-fluffy white bath sheets, then fell, naked and pink-skinned, back into bed.

An hour later he was still wide awake.

Swearing, he rose, pulled on his black silk robe, made himself some very strong coffee and trudged downstairs to his darkroom where he surprised himself by working like a demon for several hours. It was light when he emerged, but by this time he was too exhausted to care. He went upstairs, switched off his mobile, took his other phone off the hook, closed the roller shutter which he'd recently installed on his bedroom window and collapsed into bed.

If his oblivion was ravaged by erotic dreams, he certainly didn't recall them, but he was embarrassingly erect when he was wrenched out of his blissful coma by the sound of his front doorbell ringing. It was just as well, Rafe decided as he struggled out of bed, that the robe he was still wearing provided discreet coverage. Because he had no intention of getting dressed. He was going to get rid of whoever was at the door, then go back to bed for the rest of the day.

It was Isabel, looking as if she was on her way to afternoon tea with the Queen.

Cream linen trouser suit. Blue silk top. Pearls. Pink lipstick. And that lovely blonde hair of hers, slicked back up in that prissy roll thing.

Her perfect grooming highlighted his own dishevelled appearance. Why couldn't he have any luck with this woman?

'I presume you've come for your phone,' he grumped.

She looked him up and down with about the same expression she had when she'd first arrived yesterday. 'Sorry to get you out of bed,' she said drily. 'But it *is* two in the afternoon.'

Rafe decided there was no point in telling her the truth, that he'd worked most of the night because of her.

'Yeah well, we party animals do get tired. And last night *was* Saturday night. I didn't get to bed till dawn.'

'Alone?'

He crossed his arms. 'Such a personal question for a lady who's just come for her phone.'

'*You* said I'd just come for my phone. *I* didn't.'

Rafe stared at her. Was he about to get lucky here?

'Do you think I might come inside?' she went on in that silkily cool voice of hers, the one which rippled down his spine like a mink glove.

'Be my guest,' he said eagerly, stepping back to wave her inside.

'I need to go to the bathroom,' she said straight away. 'I've just driven straight down from Gosford Hospital.'

Rafe frowned as he swung the front door shut behind

him. 'What were you doing up there?' And, even more to the point, what was she doing *here*? The suburb of Paddington was not on the way from the Central Coast to her address at Burwood. So she wouldn't have dropped in just to use his toilet!

His heart was already thudding with carnal hopes.

'Luke was in a car accident on the F3 freeway yesterday,' she said.

'Is he all right?'

'A few bumps and bruises. Nothing too serious. But he knocked his head and was unconscious for a while. The police found my number in his car and contacted me early this morning, so of course I had to go and see how he was.'

'He's having some rotten luck on the road lately, isn't he? First his parents and now him. Does his new girl-friend know about this?'

'Yes, I was there when she arrived. With her mother.'

'The infamous mother. What was she like?'

'The bathroom first, please, Rafe?'

'Oh, yes—yes, of course. This way.' He had the presence of mind to take her upstairs, instead of to the small downstairs toilet. The main bathroom upstairs was quite spacious and luxurious, another recent renovation. He'd been steadily renovating his terraced home since he'd bought it a couple of years back. It had cost him a small fortune, despite being little more than a dump. But, as in all big cities, you paid for position.

After showing her where the bathroom was, he dashed into his bedroom to dress. Hurrying into his walk-in robe, he ran his eye along the hangers, wondering what to wear. The day wasn't hot, but neither was it cold. Lately they'd had typical spring weather in Sydney, fresh in the morning but warming up as the day progressed, provided it wasn't cloudy. And it wasn't today, judging by the sunshine on his doorstep just now.

By the time Isabel emerged from the bathroom Rafe was looking and feeling a bit better in his favourite black jeans and a fresh white T-shirt. But his face still sported a two-day stubble and his feet were bare.

There was only so much a man could achieve in just over three minutes, the time it took for Isabel to emerge. Clearly she wasn't a girl who titivated.

'Nice bathroom,' she said crisply.

He'd known she'd like it. It was all white, with glass and silver fittings. Cool and classy-looking, like she was.

'You might not like this room as much,' he said as he led her into his main living room, which was decorated for comfort rather than style. No traditional lounge suite, just huge squashy armchairs to sit in, functional side tables, far too many bookcases and an old marble fireplace which he never used, although the mantelpiece was good for leaning on and holding glasses during a party. He had a hi-fi set in one corner and a television and video in the other.

'I like the doors,' Isabel said, as she sat in his favourite armchair, a reclining one covered in crushed claret-coloured velvet.

He glanced at the white-painted French doors which led out onto the small terrace. 'They're purely decorative,' he said. 'I never open them because of the traffic noise.'

'What a pity.'

He shrugged. 'You can't have everything.'

'No,' she agreed with a touch of bitterness in her voice. 'You certainly can't.'

Rafe sank down in a cream leather armchair facing her, and tried to guess at why she'd come to see him.

'The mother was stunningly good-looking for a woman of forty plus,' she said abruptly. 'And the daughter was...well, let me just say that I don't think Luke is going to have a change of heart and marry me after all.'

'Were you seriously hoping he would?'

'Stupidly, I think I was beginning to. Which is really pathetic. But on the drive back to Sydney today I decided I had to stop hoping for some man to come along and give me what I want out of life. I have to go out and get it for myself. And if it's not quite what I've dreamt about all these years, if I have to compromise, then that's just the way life is.'

'That sounds sensible,' Rafe said, even though he had no idea exactly what she meant. 'So what is it you're going to do? And where do I come into the equation?'

She smiled. She actually smiled. Only a small, wry little smile, but it was even better than he'd imagined. Or worse. He'd do anything she asked of him, *be* anything she wanted him to be. If only she'd let him make love to her.

'The thing is, Rafe, I've always wanted a baby,' she announced baldly and Rafe nearly died of shock.

Hold it there, buddy, he reassessed. Now that was one thing he *wasn't* going to do, even if it did mean he'd get to do what he wanted to do most at that moment.

'Naturally, I would prefer to have a husband,' she went on, with an elegant shrug of her slender shoulders, 'or at least a live-in partner before having a child.'

'Naturally,' he said with heavy emphasis.

'But that's simply not going to happen in my case in the near future, and time is running out for me. So I've decided to opt for artificial insemination from a clinic which supplies well-documented but anonymous donors.'

Rafe was both relieved and confused. Why was she telling him all this?

'Now that Luke is going to make me an independent woman of means, I don't need a man's financial support to have a child,' she elaborated. 'I can well afford to raise one on my own. I could put the child in daycare and go back to work, if I so desired. Or hire a nanny. Of course, I do realise it's not an ideal situation, but then, it's not an ideal world, is it?'

'No,' Rafe agreed. 'But why are you telling me all this, Isabel?' he finally asked.

'I'm just filling you in on my plans so you can understand the reasons behind the proposition I am going to make you.'

'And what proposition is that?'

'I want you to come to Dream Island with me on the honeymoon Luke and I booked.'

Rafe tried not to gape. 'Er...run that by me again?'

'You heard me,' she said in a straight-down-the-line, no-nonsense fashion.

Rafe stared at her. Wow. Talk about a shock.

He might have been ecstatic if he hadn't been just a tad wary. The thought that she might have some sneaky plan to use his sperm to impregnate herself without his knowing did not escape him. Though, if that was the case, why tell him about her intention to have a baby at all? Better to keep that a secret if that had been her hidden agenda.

'Why?' he demanded to know.

'Well, it isn't because I don't want to waste money,' she threw at him with a measure of exasperation. 'Even though the honeymoon package was all prepaid and it's too late to cancel. I *want* you to come with me because I want you to come with me.'

Rafe had difficulty embracing the possibility that she just wanted him for sex, even though it was the most exciting thought. All his fantasies of the night before coming true!

'As what, exactly?' he persisted. 'If you think I'm going to pretend to be your husband as a salve to your pride, then you can think again.'

'Don't be ridiculous. I wouldn't insult you like that. You'll be with me as my...my lover.'

Mmm, she'd choked a bit over that last word. He stared deep into her eyes and tried to see what was in her mind.

'Yes, but is my role as lover just a pretend one, or do I get to have the real thing with you?'

She blushed, and it enchanted him as much as it had the first time. It also didn't gel with her wanting him as little more than a toy boy. She just didn't seem to be that kind of girl.

'Spell it out for me, Isabel. I might be being dense but I'm still not getting the full picture here.'

She sucked in deeply, then let the air out of her lungs very slowly, as though she was gathering the courage to say what she had to say. He watched her, fascinated and intrigued.

Isabel hadn't thought it would be as difficult as this. When she'd made the decision on the drive down to ask Rafe to come away with her, she'd thought it would be easy. He'd just say yes and that would be that. She hadn't anticipated that he'd question her so closely, or make her confess her desire for him quite so bluntly.

It was embarrassing, and almost…shameful.

Yet why *should* she be ashamed? came the resentful thought. Had Luke been ashamed, taking what he wanted? At least she wasn't guilty of jumping into bed with Rafe the same day she met him, or while she was engaged to someone else. They wouldn't be breaking anyone's heart by going away together.

Not that Luke had broken her heart exactly. But he'd certainly shattered her dreams.

Isabel cleared her throat, determined not to start waffling, and doubly determined not to feel one scrap of shame!

'The bottom line is this, Rafe. Just because I've decided to have a baby alone doesn't mean I always want to be alone. I happen to like sex. Actually, I like it a lot. Perversely, I seem to like it most with men like you.'

Rafe's eyebrows shot upwards, then drew darkly together. 'Hey, hold it there. What do you mean by men like me? That sounded like an insult.'

Isabel winced. She hadn't worded that at all well. 'It wasn't meant to be an insult. It was just a fact. I'm always attracted to men who aren't into commitment. That used to be a big problem, given I wanted marriage and a family. It was the main reason I decided on a marriage of convenience with Luke, because I was sick and tired of falling in love with Mr Wrong. Now that I've made the decision to have a baby on my own, I don't have to worry about the intentions of the men I sleep with, because I won't want to marry them. I just want to have sex with them. Is there some problem with that? I thought that was what you wanted, too.'

Rafe frowned. He'd thought that was what he wanted, too.

'I guess I still like my girlfriends to think I'm an okay guy, not some selfish sleazebag who uses women for one thing and one thing only.'

'Oh, but I don't want to be your girlfriend, Rafe. After the honeymoon holiday is over, I don't want to ever see you again.'

He was truly taken aback. 'But why not?'

Isabel was not about to tell him the truth on this occasion—that she didn't want to push her luck by spending too much time with him. It was one thing to live out a fantasy fortnight with him on Dream Island, quite another to have him popping around all the time after they came back to Sydney. He really was too nice a guy to allow that. She was sure to end up wanting more from him that he could give.

Right at this moment, however, she just wanted him for sex, and nothing more. One look at his gorgeously rakish self on his doorstep this morning had confirmed that. Isabel didn't want to risk changing that status quo.

'I have my reasons, Rafe,' she said firmly. 'This is a take-it-or-leave-it proposition. I'm sure I could find someone else to go with me if you turn me down.'

The thought of her going with someone else made up Rafe's mind in a hurry. 'No need to do that,' he said hurriedly. 'I'd love to go with you.'

'On my terms and no questions asked?' she insisted.

'None except essentials. Firstly, how long will I be away?'

'Two weeks.'

Two weeks. Fourteen days and fourteen nights. Fantastic! 'And it's on Dream Island.'

'Yes, you've been there before?'

'No, but I've heard about it.' It was the newest and most exclusive of the tropical island resorts off the far North Queensland coast, specialising in romantic holidays for couples and honeymooners. He wondered if they would have one of the special bures overlooking their own private beach. That would be really something. To be totally alone with her with nothing to do but eat, sleep, swim and make love. His kind of holiday!

'When, exactly, do we fly out?' he asked eagerly.

'Today fortnight, at ten in the morning. I'll pick you up here at eight. Be ready.' She stood up abruptly.

'Hey.' He jumped up also. 'You're not leaving, are you?'

'I have no reason to stay any longer,' she returned, her manner firm. 'You said yes. We have nothing more to discuss.'

'What about contraception?'

She stared hard at him. 'I presume I can rely on you to see to that.'

'You're not on the pill?'

'No, and even if I was I would still want you to use condoms.'

He supposed that was only sensible, but he still felt mildly insulted. Which was crazy, really.

'Fine,' he said. 'But there's still no reason to rush off, is there? I mean...fair enough if you don't want to see me afterwards, but it might be nice to spend some time together *before* we go off on holiday together. Get to know each other a little better.'

'I'm sorry but I don't want to do that.'

'Why not, for pity's sake?'

'Look, Rafe, may I be blunt?'

Did she know any other way? 'Please do,' he bit out.

'We both know what the term 'getting to know you' means in this day and age. No, please don't deny it. I'm being brutally honest with you and I would appreciate the same in return. Aside from the fact my period is due this week and I'm suffering considerably from PMT right now, I simply don't want us to go to bed together beforehand.'

'Why not?'

She gave him another of those small enigmatic smiles. 'Maybe I don't want to risk you finding me a disappointment in bed and running a mile.'

Never in a million years, he thought. She only had to lie there and he'd be enchanted. Anything more was a bonus. But, since she openly confessed to liking sex, then he figured she was going to do more. How *much* more was the intriguing part.

'Don't *you* want to try before you buy?' he said with a saucy smile, and she laughed.

'I've seen all I need to see. You really shouldn't come to your front door half asleep and half dressed, Rafe darling. Now, show me where you put my phone, please. It's high time I went home.'

CHAPTER SEVEN

RAFE paced the front room, waiting for Isabel to arrive. She'd said she'd pick him up right on eight. But it was eight-ten and she hadn't shown up yet.

Maybe she wasn't going to. Maybe this had all been some kind of sick joke, revenge against the male sex.

This ghastly thought had just occurred to Rafe when he heard a car pulling up outside. Peeping out through the front window, he was relieved to see that it was her. Snatching up his luggage, he was out of the door before she could blow the horn. By the time he'd reached her car she'd alighted and was waiting beside the hatchback for him, looking gorgeous in pink pedal-pushers, a pink and white flowered top, and sexy white slip-on sandals. Her lipstick was bright pink, her hair was bouncing around her shoulders and her perfume smelt of freshly cut flowers.

'Sorry I'm a bit late,' she apologised as she looked him up and down. Without contempt this time. 'I had this sudden worry that you might have forgotten some essential items so I stopped off at a twenty-four hour chemist on the way.'

He grinned at her. 'Not necessary. They were the first thing I packed. But no worry. We won't run out now, will we? Which might have been a possibility if you're going to look as delicious as you look this morning all the time. Love the pink. Love the hair. But I especially love that perfume.'

Isabel tried not to let her head be turned by his compliments. Men like Rafe were always good with the charm.

At the same time, she'd come here today determined to enjoy what he had to offer. Cancelling everything for the wedding had been infinitely depressing, as had Luke's call telling her that he and Celia were now officially engaged. Isabel was in quite desperate need to be admired and desired, both of which she could see reflected in Rafe's gorgeous brown eyes.

'It's new,' she told him brightly. 'So are the clothes. I splashed out.'

That had been the only positive thing to happen during the last fortnight—Luke coming good with his promise to set her up financially. To give him credit, he hadn't let the grass grow under his feet in that regard. Guilt, no doubt.

Still, she was now the proud owner of a brilliant portfolio of blue-chip stock and shares, the deed to the Turramurra town house and a bonus wad of cash, some of which she'd recklessly spent on a wild new resort wardrobe. She'd given the more conservative clothes she'd bought to take on her honeymoon with Luke to Rachel, who was grateful, but wasn't sure where she'd ever get to wear them.

'You should splash out more often,' Rafe told her. 'I like the less formal you.'

'And I've always liked the less formal you,' she quipped back.

He was wearing fawn cargo slacks and a multi-coloured Hawaiian shirt, his bare feet housed in brown sandals. He must have shaved some time since she last saw him, but not that morning. Still, he looked and smelt shower-fresh, his silver phantom earring sparkling in the sunshine.

He smiled and rubbed a hand over his stubbly chin. 'You could have fooled me. So you like it rough, do you?'

'No lady would ever answer such a question,' she chided in mock reproof.

'And no gentleman would ask it,' he said, smiling cheekily. 'Happily for you, I'm no gentleman.'

'I'm sure you have your gentle side. Now, stop with the chit-chat and put your bag in here. If we don't get going we'll miss the plane.'

'Nah. At this hour on a Sunday morning we'll be at the airport in no time flat. The plane doesn't go till ten, does it?' he asked as he swung his one suitcase in beside her two.

'No,' she said, and slammed the hatchback down.

'Then we have time for this.'

When he pulled her abruptly into his arms, Isabel stiffened for a second. But only for a second. What was the point in making some silly show of resisting? This was why she found him so attractive, wasn't it? Because this was the kind of thing he would do.

Not like Luke. Luke always asked. He never took. Luke was a gentleman.

Not such a gentleman with Celia, however. He'd whisked her into bed before you could say Bob's your uncle! A matter of chemistry, Isabel realised.

As Rafe's lips covered hers, Isabel knew the chemistry between *them* was similarly explosive.

Sparks definitely flew and her head spun.

This was what she craved! Forceful lips and an even more forceful tongue. She leant into him, wanting more. She moaned before she could stop herself.

Rafe was startled by her response. The way she melted against him. The way she moaned. Wow, this was no ice princess. This was one hot babe he had in his arms!

When his head lifted, she made a small sound of protest.

He gave her one final peck on her wetly parted lips before putting her away from him. 'I can see this is going to be one fantastic holiday, honey,' he murmured throatily. 'But perhaps you're right. Perhaps we should get going before we really do miss that plane.'

Isabel hoped she wasn't blushing. She'd done enough blushing since meeting this man. Blushing was for female fools. And wishy-washy wimps. Not for a woman who'd decided to fashion her own destiny in every way.

So Rafe turned her on with effortless ease. Good. That was his job for the next fortnight.

But what about after that? she wondered, throwing him a hungry glance as she climbed back in behind the wheel. Mmm, she would see. Maybe she would keep his number in her little black book for the occasional night of carnal pleasure. Depending on how good he was at the real thing. If his kissing technique was anything to go by, she was in for some incredible sex.

Rafe didn't know quite what to make of the smug little smile which crossed that pink mouth.

Frankly, he didn't know what to make of Ms Isabel Hunt at all!

But he wasn't going to worry about it. He'd lost enough sleep over her this last two weeks. The next fortnight was going to be a big improvement, particularly in the insomnia department. He always slept like a log after sex.

'So, who did you tell your mother you were going away with?' he asked as soon as they were on their way.

She slanted him a curious look. 'What makes you sure I told her anything?'

'I have a mother,' he said drily. 'I know what they're like. They want to know the ins and outs of everything. Often, you have to resort to little white lies to keep them happy. I keep telling my mother that the only reason I haven't married is because I haven't met the right girl yet.'

'And that works for you?'

'I have to confess it's losing its credibility. I think by the time I'm forty she'll resort to taking out ads for me in the newspapers. You know the kind. ''Attractive single male seeks companionship view matrimony from attractive single female. Must be able to cook well and like children.'''

'If she does, I might answer. I cook very well and I adore children.'

'Very funny, Isabel. Now answer the question. Who is supposed to be going with you?'

'Rachel.'

'Who's Rachel?'

'My best friend. The one who was going to wear my wine-red bridesmaid gown.'

'And your mother *believed* you were taking a woman to Dream Island with you?'

'Yes.'

'Wow. My mother would never have believed that.'

'That you were taking a woman to Dream Island?'

'My, aren't we witty today?'

She smiled. 'Amongst other things.'

'What other things?'

'Excited. Are you excited, Rafe?'

He stared over at her. What was he getting himself into here? Whatever it was, it was communicating itself to that part of himself which he'd been trying to control for fourteen interminable days and nights.

'That's putting it mildly,' he confessed.

Her head turned and their eyes locked for a moment. He'd never felt a buzz like it. He could hardly wait.

But wait he had to. For two hours at the airport when the plane to Cairns was delayed. Then another short delay at Cairns for the connecting helicopter flight to Dream Island.

It was almost five in the afternoon by the time they landed on the heliport near the main reception area of the resort, then another hour before they were transported by luxury motor boat to—*yes*! Their own private bure on their own private beach!

Rafe was over the moon. Talk about fantasies coming true!

As he helped Isabel from the boat onto the small jetty, he glanced up at where the bure was set, on the lushly covered hillside on a natural terrace overlooking the water. Hexagon-shaped, it looked quite large, with what looked like an outdoor sitting area, a fact confirmed as they came closer. There was even a hammock strung between two nearby palm trees. Rafe eyed it speculatively when they walked past, wondering what it would be like to make love in a hammock.

The young chap named Tom who'd brought them there in the boat took them through the place, explaining all the mod cons which were state of the art, especially in the bathroom. The spa was huge. There was no expense spared with the white cane furniture and linen furnishings either, all in bright citrus colours with leafy tropical patterns.

No air-conditioning, Tom pointed out. Apparently that didn't work well in the humidity. But the bure had a high-domed ceiling and quite a few fans. Rafe wasn't sure how comfortable visitors would be in the height of summer, but at this time of year the climate was very pleasant, especially with the evening sea breeze which was at that moment wafting through the open doors and windows.

The bed, Rafe noted, had a huge mosquito net above

it on a frame which they were warned should be used every night. If they wanted to sit outside in the evenings, they were to spray themselves with the insect repellent provided and light the citronella-scented candle lamps dotted around.

Holidaying in the tropics, it seemed, did have some hazards.

'Because of all your travelling today,' Tom told them, 'the manager thought you'd be too tired to return to the main resort for dinner, so he had the chef pack you that special picnic dinner.' And he nodded towards the large basket he'd placed on the table in the eating nook.

'The refrigerator and cupboards are well stocked with more food and wine. The bar in the corner over there has every drink on its shelves you could possibly imagine. As I'm sure you are aware, all drink and food is included in the tariff here, so please don't stint yourself. Each day, you can either eat in the various restaurants in the hotel on the main beach or have something sent over. You only have to ring for service. Cigarettes are included also, if you smoke.'

'We don't smoke,' Isabel said for both of them, before frowning up at Rafe. 'You don't, do you?' she whispered and he shook his head.

'I'll be going, then,' Tom said crisply. 'There are brochures on the coffee-table explaining all the resort's facilities. You have your own little runabout attached to the jetty which I will show you how to operate before I leave. You must understand, however, that you can't walk to anywhere from here, except up to the top of the hill we're on. The path is quite steep from this point, but the view's pretty spectacular, especially at sunrise. Worth the effort at least once. I think that's all, but if you have any questions you only have to pick up the phone and ring Reception. Now, if you'd like to come with me, sir, I'll show you how to start the runabout's motor and how to steer.'

Isabel watched them leave, then walked over and sat down on the side of the bed, testing it for comfort. It was firm. Luke's bed had been firm, she recalled.

Luke...

He'd rung her yesterday and told her he and Celia were getting married in a couple of months. For a honeymoon, he was going to take her around the world. For a whole year. After that, they were going to start trying for a baby.

Isabel didn't envy Celia the trip. She'd travelled a lot herself. Saved up during her twenties and gone to those places she'd always thought exotic and romantic. Paris. Rome. Hawaii.

But she envied her that baby. And Luke as its father. He was going to make a truly wonderful father.

Suddenly, all her earlier excitement faded and she wanted to cry. Before she knew it she *was* crying, tears flooding her eyes and overflowing down her cheeks.

Isabel dashed them away with the back of her hands, angry with herself. If only she hadn't let Luke go racing off to Lake Macquarie that Friday. If only she hadn't been so darned reasonable she would have been here tonight, with him. They would have been married, and she would have been making a baby in this bed. Or at least trying to.

Instead, she was here with Rafe!

Throwing herself onto the bed, Isabel buried her face in the mountain of pillows and wept.

Rafe was taken aback when he walked back in and found Isabel crying on the bed. He hated hearing women cry. His mother had cried for a long time after his Dad had been killed. It had upset Rafe terribly, listening to her sob into her pillows every night.

'Hey,' he said softly, and touched Isabel's trembling shoulder.

With a sob, she turned her back to him and curled up into a ball on the green-printed quilt. 'Go away,' she cried piteously. 'Just go away.'

Rafe didn't know what to do. He hadn't a clue what was wrong. She'd said she hadn't loved her fiancé. Had she lied? Had she taken one look at this place and this bed and wanted not him, but Luke?

Dismayed, Rafe went to leave, but then decided against it. She shouldn't be left alone like this. She needed him, if only to comfort her for now.

He lay down on the bed and wrapped his arms around her from behind. 'It's all right, sweetheart,' he soothed, holding her tightly against him. 'I understand. Honest, I do. I'll bet you've been holding your hurt in this last fortnight, and now that you're here, where you should have been with Luke, his dumping you for that Celia girl has hit you hard. Look, I know what it's like to be chucked over for someone else. And it's hell. So cry all you want to. I did.'

Talking to her and touching her seemed to do the trick. Her weeping subsided to a sniffle and she turned over in his arms to stare up at him. 'You did?'

'Yep. Maybe it's not the done thing for a bloke to blubber, but I was like Niagara Falls for a day or two. Heck, no, longer than that. I was a mess on and off for a week. I didn't dare go out anywhere. It was most embarrassing. I drank like a fish too, but that didn't help at all. Made me even more maudlin.'

'Why did she dump you?'

'Ambition. And money. And influence. Be assured it wasn't because the other chap was better in bed,' Rafe added with a grin, and she laughed. It was a lovely sound.

He took advantage of the moment and kissed her. Not the way he'd kissed her back in Sydney this morning, but slowly, softly, sipping at her lips, showing her with his mouth that he *did* have a gentle side. He kept on kissing her, nothing more, and gradually he felt her defences lower till finally she began to moan, and move against him. Only then did he start to undress her—and himself—still taking his time, touching and talking to her as he went, reassuring her of how much he admired and desired her.

It wasn't easy, keeping his head, especially when he uncovered her perfect breasts and sucked on their perfect and very pert nipples, but he managed, till they were both totally naked and she was trembling for him.

It almost killed him to leave her and go get a condom. But a man had to do what a man had to do.

He was quick. Real quick. After all, he'd been slipping on condoms for years. Though rarely when he'd been as excited as this. Had he *ever* been as excited as this, even with Liz?

Maybe his memory was defective but he didn't think so. This was a one-off experience, perhaps because Isabel had made him wait two weeks to consummate what she'd evoked in him the first time he'd looked at her. This was lust at its most tortuous. And frustration at its most fierce.

He was thankful she felt the same way.

Or so he'd thought, till he hurried back to the bed and saw her looking at him with something like fear.

But why would she be afraid of him?

'What is it?' he asked as he joined her on the bed once more and drew her back into his arms. 'What's worrying you?'

'Nothing,' she said, shaking her head. 'Nothing.'

'Is it still Luke?'

'No. No!'

'Is it me, then? You're worried I might hurt you.'

She blinked her surprise at his intuition.

'Oh, honey, honey,' he murmured. 'I would never hurt you. I just want to make you happy, to see you smile and hear you laugh again. I want to give you pleasure. Like this,' he said as he stroked her legs apart, his fingers knowing exactly where to go and what to do.

She gasped while he groaned. How wet she was. It

was going to feel fantastic, being buried to the hilt in that.

Waiting any longer was simply not on. And possibly counter-productive. He would feel safer inside her. Less tense. He might even relax a bit.

As though reading his mind, she shifted her thighs apart and bent her knees, inviting him in, murmuring yes in his ear over and over. His fingers fumbled a fraction as he sought to push his suddenly desperate flesh into hers.

Rafe sighed with relief, then just wallowed in blissful stillness for a few seconds. But any respite was short-lived.

As soon as he began to move, her legs were around him like a vine. Or was it a vice? She was squeezing him with her heels and with her insides, rocking back-ward and forward.

Rafe felt a wild rush of blood along his veins, swelling him further, compelling him to pump harder as he sought release from his agony.

And he'd thought he'd be more relaxed inside her.

Foolish Rafe!

'Rafe,' she cried out, her arms tightening around his neck, her lips breathing hot fire against his throat. 'Rafe...'

Her first spasm sent him into orbit, to a place he hadn't known existed. Was it pleasure or pain as his seed was wrenched from his body? Agony or ecstasy as her almost violent contractions kept milking him dry, mak-ing him moan as he'd never moaned before.

Rafe didn't know if he was experiencing happiness, or humiliation. All he knew was that no sooner did he feel himself falling away from that place she'd rocketed him to, than he wanted to be there again.

'You're right,' she murmured, kissing his throat and stroking his back, his shoulders, his chest. 'You didn't hurt me.'

His eyes opened to stare down at her.

'You looked so big,' she explained breathily. 'I haven't been with a man that big before.'

Rafe was startled. He'd always thought of himself as pretty average. What she'd been seeing was mostly *her* doing. Still, he was secretly flattered.

'I'd thought you were worried I might hurt you emotionally,' he said.

'Oh, no,' she said, shaking her head. 'No, that won't happen. I won't ever let that happen.'

Now Rafe felt piqued. Which was crazy. She'd spelled out what she wanted when she'd propositioned him and he'd agreed. Sex on tap for a fortnight without any strings and without any follow-up.

He'd thought such a set-up was every man's fantasy come true. Now, for some reason that he hadn't anticipated, Rafe wasn't so sure.

Oh, for pity's sake, stepped in the voice of cold reason. What's got into *you*? This *is* every man's fantasy come true. Stop playing the sensitive New Age guy and start being exactly what she thinks you are. Rafe the rake!

The trouble was Rafe wasn't really a rake. Never had

been. Still, it might be fun. He could do every outrageous thing he'd ever wanted to do and get away with it. Make the most wicked suggestions. Play Casanova to the hilt, with a bit of the Marquis de Sade thrown in.

He had to smile at that. Him, into bondage and stuff? Wasn't his usual cup of tea, but that hammock had possibilities...

'Why are you smiling like that?' she asked.

'Like what?'

'Like the cat who got the cream.'

'Perhaps because I just did. You are the best in bed, sweetheart. Simply the best.'

She looked slightly uncomfortable with his compliment, as though she didn't like her performance being rated. Yet she must know she was good at sex.

She was a complex creature, and a maze of contradictions. Cool and ladylike on the surface whilst all this white-hot heat was simmering away underneath.

Rafe aimed to keep her furnace well stoked for the next fortnight. She wasn't going to be allowed to retreat into that ridiculous touch-me-not façade, not for a moment. She might think she'd hired him as her private toy boy, but in fact *she* was the one going to be the toy, to be played in whatever way he fancied.

Rafe might have been shocked by the wickedness of his thoughts under normal circumstances. But these were hardly normal circumstances, and it was what she wanted, after all.

'Hey, but I'm hungry,' he said. 'Aren't you?'

'A little. But I could do with a shower first. We've been travelling all day.'

'Mmm. Me, too. But why have a shower when there's that lovely big spa? We could pop in together. What say we take that picnic basket with us as well, kill two birds with one stone?'

'But…'

'But, nothing, honey. You just do what good old Rafe tells you and you'll have the time of your life.'

CHAPTER EIGHT

RAFE was right, Isabel thought two days later. She *was* having the time of her life. He was exactly what she needed just now.

Oversexed, of course. He never left her alone.

But she wasn't complaining. If she was brutally honest, she wanted him as much as he wanted her. He was wonderfully flirtatious and fun, with just the right amount of bad boy wickedness to his lovemaking which she'd always found exciting.

'So what do you think?' she said as she modelled her new red bikini for him.

Rafe was still sitting on the terrace in the morning sunshine, partaking in the slowest, longest breakfast. He was naked to the waist, a pair of colourful board shorts slung low around his hips. He was all male.

His eyes lifted and he stared at her. She hadn't worn this particular swimming costume for him as yet and it was scandalously brief. All the swimwear she'd bought with Luke's money was scandalous in some way, selected in a mood of rebellion and defiance.

And with Rafe in mind.

The white one-piece she'd worn yesterday went totally transparent when wet. Swimming had come to a swift end on that occasion, which was perhaps just as well, since her fair skin couldn't take too much sun. As it was, she was slightly pink. All over.

'Turn round,' he ordered.

She did, knowing full well what the sight of her bottom in nothing but a thong would do to him. Still, that was the general idea. She'd been like a cat on a hot tin roof since he'd come up behind her as she'd been setting out breakfast on the terrace an hour ago, and proceeded to have her right then and there, out in the open. No foreplay whatsoever. Just him, whispering hot words in her ear as he lifted the hem of the sarong she was wearing, then commanding her to stand perfectly still whilst he quite selfishly took his pleasure.

She'd nearly spilled the jug of orange juice she'd been holding at the time. She hadn't come, of course. He'd been much too fast and she'd been much too tense. It had left her terribly turned on, though. She was still turned on an hour later. Hence the red bikini.

Isabel hadn't brought Rafe along with her to remain frustrated for long.

When he said nothing, she spun back round and glared at him, her hands finding her hips.

'Well, what do you think?'

'I think you should come over here,' he said, and downed the rest of his orange juice.

A quiver ran all through her as she walked towards him. What was he going to do to her? Or make her do to him?

When he handed her the empty glass, she just stared at him.

'What's this?' she said.

'I've finished. I thought you might like to clear the table.'

'Then you thought wrong,' she snapped.

'In that case, what do you want to do? Or should I say, what is it you want *me* to do to *you*? If you tell me in minute explicit detail, Isabel, I'll do it exactly as you describe. Anything you want, honey. Anything at all.'

Her mouth had gone dry. '*Anything*?'

'Uh-huh.'

'I…I don't know what I want…'

He took the empty glass out of her hands, put it back on the table, then drew her down onto his lap. 'Yes you do,' he murmured as he moved aside the tiny triangles which barely covered her breasts and began playing with her nipples. 'You know exactly what you want.'

'I…' She could hardly think with him doing what he was doing. Her nipples had tightened into twin peaks of heightened sensitivity, and he was rolling them with his fingertips in exquisite circles.

'Tell me,' he said, his breath hot in her ear. 'Tell me…'

She shuddered and squirmed. 'No,' she croaked. 'No, I can't.'

'Why not?'

'It's…it's too embarrassing.'

'Then I'll tell you what you want. You want me to give you a climax first. With my tongue. You want *me* to wait this time, till I'm climbing the walls like I was our first time together. Even then, you want to torment me some more with this sexy mouth of yours.'

His right hand lifted from her aching nipples to touch her lips, making them gasp apart. She automatically sucked in when he slipped a finger inside.

'Yes, just like that,' he said thickly, sliding his finger in and out of her mouth. 'You'd like to do that to me, wouldn't you, Isabel?'

She shuddered all over.

'And then,' he went on in a low seductive whisper, 'you want me to do it to you like there's no tomorrow. You want me to scatter your mind, to make you feel nothing but the wild heat of the moment, and the beautiful blissful oblivion that will follow afterwards.'

When his hot words finally stilled, so did that finger. A charged silence descended, with no sounds but the heaviness of his breathing and the waves on the beach.

Isabel wasn't breathing at all!

Suddenly, his chair scraped back and he was up and carrying her, not over to the bure and the bed, as she was desperately hoping, but down the path which led to the beach. She was startled when he dumped her into the hammock on the way past then continued on himself to run across the sand and plunge into the ocean. Meanwhile, she had to clutch wildly at the sides of the swinging hammock to stop herself from falling out.

When he returned less than a minute later, all wet and smiling, she threw him the blackest look. 'You did that deliberately, didn't you?' she growled, still clutching at the hammock. 'Turned me on, then made me wait some more.'

'Nope. It just happened that way. Perversely, I turned myself on even more than I was trying to do to you. I had no idea just talking about sex like that was so powerful. Had to go cool myself off before things became downright humiliating. But I'm back now, ready and able to put my words into action. So where shall we begin, lover? Right here in the hammock?'

'Don't be silly. The darned thing won't stay still. And you don't have a condom with you.'

'I wasn't going to have actual sex with you here, Isabel,' he said drily. 'If you recall, that doesn't come till much later in the scenario I outlined, by which time I'm to carry you back to the bure.'

Her mouth gaped open. 'You…you mean you're going to do what you…d…d…described?'

'Every single bit of it. And so are you.'

Her face flamed.

'You'll like it, I promise,' he purred as he pulled her round crosswise and began peeling off her bikini bottom.

She did like it. Too much. Way too much.

But he was wrong about afterwards. He might have fallen into blissful oblivion on the bed afterwards, but she lay there wide awake, her thoughts going round and round.

She wasn't going to be able to give him up after a mere fortnight. That was the truth of it. She was going to want him around for much longer than that.

Why? That was the question. Was it the way he *could*

make her forget everything but the moment? Was it for
the brilliant and blinding climaxes he could give her? Or
was it something more insidious, something she'd
vowed never to do, ever again?

Fall in love...

Rolling over onto her side, she looked at him lying
there, sprawled naked on the lemon sheets, his arms
flung wide, his silky brown hair. Leaning forward, she
lifted one heavy lock from across his eyes and dropped
it onto the pillow, then removed another which was covering his nostrils and mouth.

As if sensing that he could now breathe more easily,
he sighed a deep, contented sigh, his mouth almost smiling in his sleep.

Isabel found herself smiling as well. Maybe she
wanted to keep him around because she just liked him.
And because he seemed to really like her in return.

Liking was good, she decided. She could live with
that.

Finally, Isabel's worries calmed, she curled up to Rafe
and went to sleep.

CHAPTER NINE

'NO RINGING for a dinner drop tonight, Isabel,' Rafe told her. 'We need to get up, get dressed and get away from here for a while. Do something else for a few hours. Have a change of scene.'

Isabel's head lifted and she smiled at him. 'Yes, Rafe darling, but surely you don't want me to get up and get dressed right at this precise moment.'

He stared back down into her cool blue eyes and wished he had the strength to tell her, yes, stop. Stop tormenting me. Stop enslaving me. Stop making me addicted to your body. And to you.

It was Wednesday, and they were back in bed, not long awake from an afternoon nap after a rather rigorous morning. They'd gone for a dawn swim after minimal sleep the night before and hadn't bothered with swimwear. There was no one to see them, after all. No one to see what they did in the water. Or on the wet sand. Or in the hammock again.

The hammock...

Rafe swallowed as he thought of what he'd done to her in the hammock last night, how he'd used the silk sarong she'd been wearing to bind her hands to the rope up above her head. He'd never done anything like that before. And neither had she, if he was any guess.

But what a sight she'd been stretched out there, naked, in the moonlight. Rafe had been incredibly turned on. And Isabel…Isabel had been beside herself. She'd come so many times he lost count. In the end, she'd begged him to stop.

But he hadn't been able to stop, not for a long long time.

And now he wasn't able to stop *her* as she drew him deep into her mouth once more.

He moaned at the heat of it. And the wetness. It was like being sheathed in molten steel. He was going to come. He knew he was going to come.

His raw cry of warning stopped her, leaving him dangling right on the edge.

'You have a problem, lover?' she drawled huskily as she reached for one of the condoms they kept beside the bed.

He choked out a rueful laugh. 'You're cruel, do you know that?'

'Now you know how I felt last night,' she said as she protected them both. 'Just as well my perfume acts as an effective insect repellent or I'd have been covered with insect bites.'

'Instead, you have a few bites of another kind.'

'Beast.'

'You loved it.'

'And you're loving this. So why don't you just lie back and enjoy?'

He sucked in sharply when she bent to take him in her mouth once more.

'No, don't,' he groaned, and her head lifted, her eyes surprised.

'No?'

'No.' He shook his head. 'Not like that.'

He reached down and pulled her up and onto him, spreading her legs outside of his, then pushing his tormented flesh inside her once more. With a primal groan he grabbed her buttocks, kneading them as he rocked her quite roughly up and down on him. They came together, backs arching, mouths gaping wide apart, bodies throbbing wildly in unison.

'Oh, Rafe,' she cried, collapsing face down across his chest, her insides still spasming.

He held her to him till she stopped, though a shudder still ran through her every now and then.

Too much, he began thinking. This is all getting too much.

'I have to go to the bathroom,' he told her a bit brusquely.

'No, don't leave me,' she begged, clinging to him.

'Sorry. Nature calls.' He was out of her and off the bed in a flash, lurching across the sea matting floor and into the bathroom. Closing the door, he leaned against it for a few air-sucking seconds before staggering over to the toilet, not really needing it except to do some essential personal housekeeping.

When he went to do just that, he stared down at himself in horror.

'Oh, no...' he muttered.

Not once had Rafe had a condom break before on him. Not once!

Till now…

His heart sinking, Rafe inspected the damage and it was the worst scenario possible. The darned thing had totally failed. Ripped asunder. Right across the tip.

Immediately he thought of Isabel and in his mind's eye he could see millions of eager little tadpoles careering through her cervix and into her womb, swimming around with more energy than the Olympic water-polo team, watching and waiting to score a home goal.

What were the odds of their doing just that? he wondered frantically, his mind scouring his memory to recall what Isabel had said to him that Sunday just over two weeks ago. Something about her period being due that week. Probably early on in the week, he guessed. She'd said something about suffering from PMT that day.

Rafe did some mental arithmetic and worked out that if Isabel was a normal regular female with a normal monthly cycle, then she had to have already entered, or be entering, her 'most likely to conceive phase' right now.

Rafe sank down on the side of the spa bath. He might have just become a father!

His head whirled. So did his stomach. She was going to kill him when he told her.

Then don't tell her, came the voice of male logic. It will only spoil everything. And there's nothing you can do about it now. Besides, it might not happen. It might not be the right time. Even if it was, couples sometimes tried for years—hitting ovulation day right on the dot—and the woman didn't fall pregnant. Let's not be paranoid about this.

But what if Isabel *had* fallen pregnant. What then?

Cross that bridge when you come to it, Rafe.

Right. Good advice.

Rafe stood up, jumped into the shower and turned on the water. Picking up the shower gel, he poured a generous pool into his hands and slapped it onto his chest.

But a *baby*, he began thinking as he washed himself. *His* baby. His and *Isabel's* baby.

Talk about the best plans of mice and men.

Isabel lay there listening to Rafe in the shower and thinking she could do with a shower herself. She felt icky. But no way was she going to join him in there, not after the way she'd just carried on, clinging to him and pleading for him to stay with her like some lovesick cow.

How typical of herself! And how humiliating!

No wonder he'd bolted out of the bed.

Rafe was right. It was high time they did something else instead of have sex. She was beginning to fall into old ways.

Isabel sighed. If only he was less skilful in the love-making department. If only he didn't know exactly the sort of thing which excited her unbearably. If only he didn't always turn the tables on her such as just now.

She'd thought she was being the boss in the bedroom, as she'd used to be sometimes with Luke, but in a flash Rafe had whipped control out of her hands and she'd become his willing little love slave again, as she'd been last night.

Isabel's face flamed as she thought how crazy it had been of her to let him tie her up like that. But, ooh, it had been so deliciously thrilling. And really, down deep, she'd never felt worried. There'd been no fear in her, only excitement.

It had been a game, an erotic game. Just as this holiday together was a game. Rafe knew that. And she knew that.

So why did she keep forgetting?

No more, she resolved. From now on she would stick to the rules. And to the agreed agenda. As for any silly idea she'd been harbouring of seeing Rafe occasionally after this fortnight was over… That was not on. Experience warned her if she saw Rafe outside of this fantasy setting she was sure to fall in love with him, or start relying on him for her day-to-day happiness. She'd been there, done that, and she wasn't ever going there again. Heaven help her, if she couldn't learn from her past mistakes!

Isabel was lying there under a sheet, feeling relatively in control once more, when Rafe emerged from the steaming bathroom, rubbing his brown hair dry with a bright orange towel, a lime-green one slung rather hazardously low around his hips.

Wow, she thought as her gaze ran hungrily over him. He really was gorgeous, even more so now that he was sporting an all-over tan. She loved the long lean look on a man, loved broad bronzed shoulders which tapered down to a small waist. *Loved* tight little buns.

Not that she could see his buns at that moment. But she had an imprint in her memory bank.

'It's time you got up, lover,' he said, draping the orange towel over his shoulder and finger-combing his hair back from his face. 'It's just gone five. I want to be gone from here by six.'

'Fine. I was just waiting for you to finish,' she replied, but, when she swung her feet over the side of the bed and sat up, Isabel hesitated. There wasn't anything for her to put on at hand. She hadn't worn any clothes all day and the sarong she'd been wearing last night was still tied to the hammock. The rest of her clothes were in the walk-in wardrobe, and it was actually further to walk over there than it was to the bathroom.

It was silly that walking around naked in front of Rafe should bother her. He'd seen every inch of her up close and personal. Too silly for words!

Gathering her courage, she tossed aside the sheet she'd been clutching and stood up, wincing a little once she started walking. Oh dear, she *was* icky. That was another thing she found a bit embarrassing. How wet she was all the time.

Not that Rafe minded. He said it was a real turn-on.

Still, once Isabel reached the shower she lathered herself up down there with some degree of over-enthusiasm, as if by removing the evidence of her ongoing heat, she could better keep her cool around him. A waste of time, she realised on remembering she had nothing to wear to dinner tonight but the choice of three highly provocative outfits, all bought to tease and tantalise, herself as well as Rafe.

Which one would do the least damage? she wondered. The little black dress?

No. It was way *too* little, halter-necked with no back and a short tight skirt which looked as if it was sewn on, owing to the material being stretchy.

What about the blue silk petticoat-style number with the swishy skirt?

No. Not with her nipples standing out all the time like ready-to-fire cannons. The material was too thin and the bodice too clingy.

It would have to be the emerald and gold trouser suit. Although still provocative, she at least got to wear a bra, of sorts. But the outfit did have other hazards. Such as the fulfilling of an old fantasy of hers to look like a harem girl. The pants were harem-style, and the emerald material semi-transparent, shot with gold thread. The outfit was only saved from indecency by being overlaid with a thigh-length jacket. The bra of sorts was a strapless corselette, heavily beaded in green and gold glass beads and designed to manoeuvre even the smallest of breasts into a cleavage. Isabel's breasts, though not large, were not small either. The result was eye-catching to say the least.

Once dressed and made-up, Isabel stared at herself in the floor-length mirror which hung on the back of the walk-in wardrobe door and thought she'd never looked sexier. Her hair was up, though not in its usual French roll. She'd just bundled it up loosely in a very casual topknot, leaving strands of various lengths to fall around her face. The long green and gold crystal earrings in her ears would swing when she walked. *If* she could walk, she amended as she squeezed her feet into the outrageously high gold sandals she'd bought to go with the outfit.

'Shake a leg in there, lover,' Rafe called out. 'It's gone six.'

With a shudder which could have been excitement or apprehension, she dragged on the gauzy green jacket, sprayed on some perfume, then went to meet her master.

Rafe was out on the terrace, admiring the view in the dusk light and thinking that this place really was a fantasy come true when Isabel emerged from the bure, looking like something out of the Arabian Nights.

'Well,' he said, smiling wryly to her as he scraped back the chair and stood up. 'If ever there was an outfit designed to turn a gay man straight, then you're wearing it tonight.'

She laughed a slightly guilty-sounding laugh. 'I didn't bring any let's-do-something-else clothes with me, I'm afraid.'

'I see,' he said drily. And he did. She was only here with him for the sex. She'd made that quite clear from the start.

And he'd been with her all the way. Till their little mishap this afternoon. Now, suddenly, everything had changed. Now, suddenly, when he looked at her, he didn't see a delicious bedmate but a possible pregnancy.

Not that he didn't still desire her. He'd have to be dead not to. It was just that other thoughts were now overriding his X-rated ones. Such as perhaps he should still tell her what had happened. It wasn't too late for her to get the morning-after pill. They had a doctor on the island, he knew. And a chemist shop. He'd read the list of services available in one of the coffee-table brochures.

But, oddly, he hated the idea of her ridding her body of his baby—if his baby *was* in there. Peculiar, really, when he'd never wanted to be a father before. He still didn't.

But *she* did. Want to be a mother, that is. She wanted one enough to have one on her own. So why not his? Better than having herself artificially inseminated. Bad idea, that.

'Rafe! Why are you just standing there, frowning at me like that? What on earth are you thinking?'

'What am I thinking?' He took her arm and started propelling her down the path towards the jetty. 'I was thinking that your idea of having a baby all by yourself is not a good one. In fact, it's a very bad one. My mother found it extremely difficult raising me by herself, and she had help for the first eight years.'

'Yes, well I can understand how raising *you* would have tried the patience of a saint,' Isabel said. 'But my baby won't be having your impossible genes, Rafe, so hopefully my job won't be quite so difficult.'

'Is that so?' Rafe smiled. He couldn't help it. Irony always amused him.

'Yes, that's so!' she pronounced haughtily.

'But if you go through with this plan of yours to be artificially inseminated with some unknown donor, then you won't have any idea what kind of genes your baby will inherit from its father. Surely even *my* genes would be better than the lucky-dip method.'

'All that will be unknown is his name and address,' she informed him somewhat impatiently. 'I will know a lot of information about the donor. A complete physical description, all aspects of his health, his level of education, plus other personality traits such as his sporting interests and hobbies. That's how I aim to choose him. I will look at the list of available donors and select the one which best fits my prerequisites.'

'Fascinating. Here, I can see you're having trouble walking in those heels. I'll carry you.' She went to object but he just swept her up into his arms and carried her across the sand towards the jetty.

'Mmm. You're as light as a feather. You know, I think you've lost weight since coming to this island. Too much exercise and not enough eating,' he said, at which she pulled a face up at him.

'We have to make sure you're in tippy-top health, you know, if you're planning to have a baby soon. Three good meals a day, and no silly dieting.'

'Yes, Dr Saint Vincent,' she mocked.

'Just talking common sense. Of course perhaps you're not serious about having a baby soon, or on your own at all. Maybe that was just talk.'

'I'm deadly serious. We're on the jetty now,' she said curtly. 'Please put me down.'

Rafe stared down into her eyes, suddenly aware of how stiffly she was holding herself in his arms. It hadn't occurred to him when he picked her up that she might be turned on by it. Whilst her vulnerability to his closeness was very flattering, taking advantage of it wasn't a priority of his at this precise moment.

He lowered her carefully onto those wicked-looking shoes. 'So tell me, Isabel, what *are* your prerequisites for choosing the father of your child?'

'No.'

'No? What do you mean, no?'

'I mean no, Rafe,' she said firmly as she marched on ahead of him out along the jetty. 'I am not going to have this conversation with you,' she threw over her shoulder. 'I wish I hadn't told you about my plans now. Why you're even interested is beyond me.'

He hurried after her. 'Oh, come on, don't be like that. If we're going to sit across the table and have dinner for a couple of hours we have to talk about something. And I'm curious.'

She spun round to look him straight in the eye. 'Why?'

'Why not?'

For a moment her eyes flashed with frustration, but then she shrugged. 'I might as well give in and tell you whatever you want to know, because you won't give up, will you? You'll get your way, like you did with the black and white photos. You're like that Chinese water torture.'

He grinned. 'I've been told that before.'

'I can imagine. But you can't have it *all* your own way *all* the time. If I'm to answer such highly personal questions then I have a few of my own I want answered.'

'Fair enough.' He had nothing to hide and, frankly, was intrigued over what she might want to know. More than intrigued. Rather pleased. Maybe she didn't want him just for sex. Maybe she wanted more, whether she admitted it to herself or not.

The prospect of having a more permanent relationship with this beautiful and spirited woman brought a rush not dissimilar to sexual arousal. He'd never been entirely happy with the thought of never seeing Isabel again after this fortnight was over, but had brushed aside any qualms over the rather cold-blooded terms she had set down because he wanted her so much.

But things were different now.

If she was carrying his child, then going their separate ways was simply not on.

Rafe couldn't stop his eyes from drifting down her body, first to her breasts—his baby was going to be very happy with *those*!—and then to her stomach—athletically flat at this moment. But he could imagine how it would look in a few months' time, all deliciously soft and rounded.

Isabel's insides contracted when she saw the direction of Rafe's eyes. He was thinking about sex again. She could tell. The way he'd just gobbled up her cleavage, and now he was undressing her further. He was making her all hot and bothered inside again, like he had when he'd been carrying her just now.

'Now you stop that!' she snapped, and his eyes jerked up to her face.

'Stop what?'

'You know what, you disgusting man. Now help me into this darned thing.'

The runabout rocked wildly when Isabel first stepped down into it, with Isabel almost tipping into the sea. 'Maybe we should have called Tom to take us over,' she said in a panicky voice as she clutched at the sides.

'If you'd just sit down in the middle of the seat, Isabel,' Rafe pointed out calmly, 'everything would be fine.'

Isabel did just that, and everything was fine, with Rafe starting up the motor as though he'd been doing it all his life, then steering her safely back to the main beach where he eased the small craft expertly into another jetty. His confidence and competence at things marine and mechanical reminded Isabel that men like Rafe *did* have their uses in life, other than to give women mind-blowing climaxes.

If she kept him coming around occasionally, he could also be called upon to change light-bulbs, put new washers in leaking taps and even mow the lawn. Now that she was a home owner she'd have to do things like that from time to time.

When he climbed up onto the jetty with his back to her she ogled his body quite shamelessly, especially those tight buns, housed as they were tonight in tight black jeans.

'Now you stop that,' he said, turning and grinning down at her.

'Stop what?' she managed to counter, but her cheeks felt hot.

'You know what, you disgusting woman.'

'I have no idea what you're talking about,' she parried. 'Now, help me out of here, and don't let me fall in the water.'

'Might do you good. Cool you down a tad.'

Isabel decided she really couldn't let him get away with mocking her. Her glance was cool as a cucumber. 'I thought you liked me hot and wet, not cold and wet.' And she swept past him.

Rafe watched her stalk off up the jetty and smiled. She was a one all right. More sassy and sexy than any woman he'd ever met.

But he had her measure. She liked him. She didn't want to but she did. That was why she was going to such great pains to put him in his place all the time. What she didn't realise was that fate might have already propelled him out of his role as temporary lover into possibly something far more permanent. Father of her child.

Mmm. That was another thing he had to check up on. What the odds were of that.

'Where are we going for dinner exactly?' she asked him when he caught up and took her arm.

'To the Hibiscus Restaurant. This way.' He guided her

along the planked walkway which connected the jetty to the main resort buildings which sat in several acres of tropical gardens just behind the beach.

Aside from the reception area, which also encompassed the island store, there was a five-star hotel nestled amongst the palms which boasted two à la carte restaurants, a buffet-style bistro, a couple of bars, a casino games room and a pool which, from the brochures, had to be seen to be believed. One of the restaurants was called the Hibiscus, named no doubt after the lovely tropical flower which grew in abundance on the island.

'I booked a table there while you were in the shower,' he told her. 'The woman on the other end of the phone said it was the most romantic of the restaurants here. I gather she thought we were honeymooners.'

'And you didn't tell her we weren't,' Isabel said drily.

'Goodness, no. That way, we were assured of a good table. She said since it was a balmy night she'd give us one of the ones on the terrace overlooking the pool.'

'Con artist,' Isabel scorned.

'Just being my usual clever charming self.'

'Arrogant and egotistical, that's what you are.'

'You like me arrogant and egotistical.'

'Only in bed.'

'People spend a third of their lives in bed. Except when they're on a pretend honeymoon. Then, they spend nearly *all* of it.'

Isabel laughed. And why not? Rafe had to be one of the most entertaining men she'd ever been with. It was impossible not to surrender to his charm, or be amused by his wit, which was wicked and dry, just the way she liked it.

'I love it when you laugh,' he said. 'You look even more beautiful when you laugh.'

'Do stop flattering me, Rafe. I might get used to it.'

'Ooh, and wouldn't that be dreadful?'

'Not so dreadful. Just unwise.'

'Why?'

She sighed as her good humour faded. 'I told you once before, Rafe. I don't want to have another relationship with a man whose idea of a relationship begins and ends in the bedroom.'

'And you think that's all I'd ever want from you?'

'Isn't it?'

'That depends.'

'On what?'

On whether you're carrying my child...

'On how good you can cook,' he quipped.

Her eyebrows shot up. 'You're saying the way to your heart is through your stomach? I don't believe it.'

'I *do* like my food. This way to the Hibiscus,' he directed on seeing an arrowed sign veering off to the right through the gardens. 'Mmm, I wonder what their wine list is like? Since there's no extra charge, I'll order a different bottle with each course.'

'I'm not going back in that tin-can with you if you've been drinking heavily,' she warned.

'Me, neither. If I feel I'm over the limit, we'll get someone else to take us back. Okay?'

'Okay.' She nodded. 'And don't encourage me to

drink too much, either. I still haven't got over the hang-over I had from my last binge.'

'Yes, but that was hard liquor. A few glasses of wine won't hurt.'

'Mmm. You'd say that. You're probably trying to get me drunk so that you can have your wicked way with me.'

He laughed. 'Honey, I don't have to get you drunk to do that.'

Isabel winced. 'I asked for that one, didn't I?'

He gave her an affectionate squeeze. 'Don't be silly. I love the way you are.'

Isabel didn't doubt it. Men had always been partial to whores.

Her stomach turned over at this last thought. She wasn't a whore, but maybe, in Rafe's eyes, she was act-ing like one. There again, maybe not. Rafe was not a narrow-minded man, and he didn't seem to be afflicted with that dreadful set of double standards which some men dragged up to make women feel guilty about their sexuality.

Her mother, however, wouldn't be impressed with the way she'd been behaving.

Isabel suppressed a groan. Why, oh why did she have to think of her mother? The woman was out of the ark when it came to her views on such things. She didn't appreciate that the world was a different world now. Marriage couldn't be relied upon any more to provide a woman with security for life. And men…men couldn't be relied upon at all!

'You've gone all quiet on me,' Rafe said worriedly.

'Just thinking.'

'Thinking can be bad for you.'

'What do you recommend?'

'Talking is good. And so, sometimes, is drinking. You could do with a measure of both.'

'You conniving devil. You just want to find out all my secrets.'

'You mean you have some?'

'Don't we all?'

'My life is an open book.'

'Huh! Any man with designer stubble and a phantom's head in his ear has to have *some* secrets.'

'Not me. What you see is what you get. If you think I'm indulging in some kind of pretentious arty-farty image with the way I look, you couldn't be more wrong. The phantom's head belonged to my father. I wear it all the time because when I look in the mirror I'm reminded of him. I don't shave every day because it gives me a rash if I do. As far as my clothes are concerned, I dress strictly for comfort, and in colours which don't stain easily. I am who I am, Isabel. And I like who I am. Can you say the same? Aah. Here we are. The Hibiscus.'

CHAPTER TEN

THE Hibiscus lived up to its recommendation, with even the indoor tables having a view of the spectacular pool, courtesy of glass walls on three sides of the restaurant.

Still, given the balmy night, it was going to be very pleasant sitting outside under the stars, and the table they were shown to *did* overlook the pool directly.

Round and glass-topped, the table was set with hibiscus-patterned place-mats, superb silverware and crystal glasses to suit every type of wine. The menus were printed with silver lettering on a laminated sheet which matched the place-mats.

After seeing them seated, the good-looking young waiter handed Rafe the wine list, then lit the lantern-style candle resting in the circular slot in the middle of the table, possibly where an umbrella would be inserted during daylight hours. The wine list was small but select, and Rafe ordered an excellent champagne to start with whilst Isabel silently studied the menu.

Even after the waiter departed she didn't glance up or say a word, leaving Rafe to regret the crack he'd made about her perhaps not liking who she was. She'd looked down-in-the-mouth ever since.

But if she was going to keep firing bullets, then she had to expect some back.

Still…he hated seeing her sad.

But what to do?

'Find anything there to tempt your tastebuds?' he asked lightly on picking up his own menu. A quick glance showed there were three choices for each course, rather like a set menu.

'I'm not that hungry, actually,' she murmured, still not looking up.

Rafe put down his menu. 'Look, I'm sorry, all right? I didn't mean to offend you.'

Now she did look up. 'Don't apologise. You're quite right. I don't think I do like who and what I am. I suspect I never have.'

'What rubbish. What's not to like, except the way you used to do your hair? I hated that. And it wasn't the real you at all.'

'The real me? And what's that, pray tell? Slut of the month?'

Rafe was truly taken aback, then annoyed with her. 'Don't you *dare* say that about yourself. So you're a sensual woman and enjoy sex. So what? That's nothing to be ashamed of.'

'If you say so,' she muttered unhappily.

'You should be jolly well proud of yourself. A lot of females would have folded after what you've been through just lately. But not you. You lifted your chin, squared your shoulders and went on. I might not agree with your decision to have a baby all alone, but I do admire the guts it took to make such a decision.'

Isabel was taken aback, both by his compliments and

his apparent sincerity. He liked her, and not just because she was good in bed.

'Good grief, Isabel, don't you ever go putting yourself down like that again. You have to be one of the most incredible women I've ever met, so stop that self-pitying nonsense and choose something to eat, or I'll lose patience with you and not even want to play sheikh to your harem girl at the end of the night.'

She laughed, her eyes sparkling with returned good humour. 'I knew I did right to ask you to come here with me. You are so…so…'

'Sensible?' he suggested when she couldn't find the right word.

She smiled. 'I was thinking more along the lines of refreshing.'

'Now, that's something I haven't been called before. Refreshing.'

'Take it as a compliment.'

'Oh, I will, don't worry.'

Her head tipped to one side as her eyes searched his face. 'You really are a nice man, Rafe Saint Vincent. And a very snazzy dresser. Love that black and white shirt. Can I borrow it some time?'

'You can borrow anything of mine you like. Sorry I can't return the compliment. I have a feeling I wouldn't look too good in any of your clothes.'

They were both smiling at each other when the waiter materialised by their side again with the champagne, which he duly poured, then asked if they'd like to order. Rafe did, with Isabel surrendering the choice to him, saying she liked the look of everything on the menu anyway and had recently used up all her decision-making powers.

He grinned and chose a Thai beef and noodle dish for an entrée and a grilled barramundi for the main, with a salad side plate.

'And mango cheesecake for dessert,' he finished up. 'We'll also be ordering more wine with each course. Do you have any half-bottles?'

'I'm sorry, sir, but we don't. However, you can order any of the wines listed by the glass.'

'Really? What happens to the rest of the bottle if no one else orders it?'

The waiter gave a small smirk as he whisked the menus away. 'It doesn't go to waste, sir. Be assured of that.'

'I'll bet,' Rafe said drily after the waiter departed. 'I'd like to be a fly on the wall of the kitchen every night after closing.'

'There are always perks to any job,' Isabel pointed out.

'Oh? And what were the perks of being a receptionist at a big city architectural firm?'

Isabel frowned. 'How did you know that was my job?'

'I found out when I rang Les and told him your wedding was off. We had quite a chat about you. He thinks you're a dish and wanted to know what I thought of you.'

'And you said?'

'I was suitably complimentary but discreet. Not a

word about this little jaunt, since it was obvious he knew your family fairly well.'

'Fancy that. Rafe Saint Vincent—the soul of discretion.'

'I have many hidden virtues.'

'Some not so hidden,' she said saucily.

'Naughty girl. But back to the original question. What perks were there in your job beside meeting multi-millionaire architects?'

'Not too many, actually. Free ball-point pens? And we won't count meeting Luke, since that didn't work out. I don't have to ask you what the perks of *your* job are. I've seen them on the walls of your office.'

Rafe frowned. 'What do you mean?'

'Oh, come now, lover, those photographs speak for themselves. They have foreplay written all over them.'

'You think I slept with all those women?'

'Didn't you?' Isabel picked up her crystal flute of champagne and began to sip.

'Heck, no. There were at least one or two who held out.'

Isabel spluttered into the glass.

'But they were lesbians.'

Isabel had to put down her glass.

'Stop it,' she choked out, and mopped up around her laughing mouth with her serviette.

'Would you like me to photograph you like that?'

Isabel swallowed. 'In the nude, you mean?'

'Good heavens, no. You saw my photographs. I never take full nudes. You can wear earrings, if you like. And those shoes.' One eyebrow arched wickedly as he peered at her sexily shod feet through the glass table. 'Oh yes, *definitely* those shoes.'

'You're teasing me.'

'Yep. I didn't bring my camera with me. Unfortunately.'

Thank Heaven, she thought. Because no doubt she would have let him photograph her *just* like that. Her behaviour with him since arriving on this island had been nothing short of outrageous.

'So!' she said, and swept up her champagne glass again. 'Tell me why you're opposed to my decision to have a baby alone.'

He smiled a wry smile. 'A change of subject, I presume. A wise move.' Just *thinking* about photographing her in nothing but earrings and those shoes was making him decidedly uncomfortable, especially since he was wearing rather tight jeans.

Rafe picked up his champagne, took a couple of sips and put his mind to answering her very pertinent question. If she hadn't brought up the subject of having a baby herself, he would have worked his way round to it. He hesitated to tell her what he *really* thought of her decision to have a baby alone by artificial insemination. She was determined anyway, and they'd just end up arguing. What he needed to know was the likelihood of her having conceived *his* child today.

'I just think it was a hasty decision, and one made on the rebound after Luke. You're still a young woman, Isabel, with well over a decade of baby-making capabilities left. You have more than enough time to find a suitable father for your baby before launching into motherhood alone. I think you should wait and see if he turns up.'

'Look, I told you. I tried finding Mr Right both with my heart and then my head and I bombed out both ways. No. I can't keep on waiting. And you're wrong about my having a lot of time. A woman might be theoretically capable of having a child right up until menopause, but the odds of her conceiving and carrying a healthy baby full term start to go downhill after she reaches thirty. No, Rafe, my biological clock is ticking and, knowing my luck, it's probably about to blow up. The time for action is now.'

Rafe had a bit of difficulty keeping a straight face. Little did Isabel know but the time for action might very well have been this afternoon!

'I see,' he muttered, dropping his eyes towards his champagne for a few seconds before looking up again. 'So if your marriage to Luke had gone ahead, you were planning to get pregnant pretty well straight away, then?'

Isabel sighed. 'Yes.'

'On this honeymoon?'

'Uh-huh. I had it all worked out, right to the very hour and the day.'

'Hard to pinpoint ovulation with that kind of accuracy, isn't it?'

'Not when you're as regular as I am, and when you've taken your temperature every day for three months.'

'And?' Rafe prompted. 'When would the critical time have been?'

'What? Oh, not till tomorrow, I think. Yes, Thursday. I do everything on a Thursday. Ovulate and get my period. Regular as clockwork, I am. Twenty-eight days on the dot. My girlfriends at work always used to envy the fact I was never taken by surprise, which was true. I used to pop into the loo at morning tea on P-day because I knew, come noon, the curse would arrive.'

'The curse?'

'That's what we women call it. You don't think it's a pleasure, do you? Oh, but this is a depressing topic. Would you mind if we changed the subject again? Let's talk about you.'

'Fine,' Rafe said, his head whirling. Thursday. Did sperm live for a full day? He was pretty sure it was possible, but she'd got up and had a shower soon afterwards. The odds weren't on his side.

Weren't on his side! Was he mad? He should have been relieved. He didn't really want to be a father, did he? *Did* he?

He looked at Isabel and realised he did. With her, anyway.

The realisation took his breath away.

He reefed his eyes away and stared down at the pool. Stared and stared and stared. And then his eyes flung wide. Who would have believed it?

'Rafe? Rafe, what's wrong? You look like you've seen a ghost or something.'

His gaze swung back to her and he almost laughed.

'I have. In a way. See that blonde frolicking down in the pool?'

'The one with the really big bazookas?'

'Yes, well she didn't have such big bazookas when I knew her. She must have had a boob job. Anyway, that's Liz—the girl I told you about. The one who dumped me.'

'Really?' Isabel was close enough to see the buxom blonde quite well, even better once she swam over and hauled herself up to sit on the edge of the pool. When she lifted her hands up to wring out her hair, her boobs looked like giant melons pressed together. Truly, they were enormous!

The grey-haired man she'd been canoodling with in the water climbed out via the ladder and walked over to where he'd left his towel. Whilst Liz looked in her late twenties, her companion was sixty if he was a day.

'Let's go, honey,' Isabel heard the man say with a salacious wink as he walked by. 'Time you earned your keep.'

'Coming, darls,' the blonde trilled back, though her face behind his back was less than enthusiastic.

'Is that the man she threw you over for?' Isabel asked, unable to keep the distaste out of her voice.

'No. I have no idea who that is, although I presume he's rich. No, the man Liz left me for was a fellow photographer. A more successful one at the time, though I'd heard rumours he had associations with some less than savoury video productions. I wondered what had become of Liz when I didn't see any more of her in the fashion world. I think the answer lies in those double D cups. A lot of models, especially ones who want fame and money too quickly, get sucked into doing things they shouldn't do. Pity. She could have been really someone. Instead, she's turned into *that*.' And he nodded towards the sight of her hurrying after her sugar-daddy, her gigantic breasts jiggling obscenely.

'You seem slightly sorry for her,' Isabel said, rather surprised.

'Oddly enough, I am.' He sounded surprised, too. 'Seeing her again, in the flesh so to speak, has given me a different perspective. And it's laid quite a few ghosts to rest.'

'You loved her a lot once, didn't you?'

'Yes. Yes, I did. Stupid, really. In hindsight, I can see she wasn't worth it, but love is blind, as they say.'

'I know exactly what you mean. I couldn't count the number of creeps and losers I've fallen for over the years. But, dear heaven, the last fellow I was involved with before Luke made the others look like saints. Still, I didn't know that when I first met him.'

'And where was that?'

'I was working my way around Australia and had taken this job as a salesgirl in a trendy little boutique on the Gold Coast which sold Italian shoes. One day, this sophisticated guy came in and I served him. He bought six pairs of shoes, just so he could spend more time with me, he said. Naturally, I was impressed.'

'Mmm. A bit naïve of you, Isabel, falling for a line like that.'

'That's me when I fall for a man. Naïve.'

'You weren't with me.'

'I was *attracted* to you, Rafe. I didn't fall for you.'

Terrific. Well, he'd asked for that one, hadn't he?

'So what happened next?'

'What do you think? He took me out to dinner that night, then straight home to bed afterwards.'

Rafe decided not to pursue that conversation further. He felt decidedly jealous of this Hal and his instant sexual success. Isabel had given him icicles the first day they'd met. Still, she *had* been a bride-to-be at that stage, and possibly still suffering from the once-bitten twice-shy syndrome after this fellow.

'So how did it end? Did he dump you?'

'No. Actually, he didn't. In a weird way I believe Hal did love me. As much as a man like that is capable of love. No, something happened and I could no longer pretend he was Mr Right.'

'Oh-oh, sounds like you found out he was already married.'

She laughed. 'If only it were as simple as that.'

'Now I'm seriously intrigued. What happened?'

'He was arrested. For drug importation and dealing. He got fifteen years.'

'Wow. And you never suspected?'

'Not for a moment. He didn't use drugs himself, and he never did any dealing in my presence. Even when he made numerous trips to Bangkok I didn't suspect. He said he was an importer. Of jewellery. I should have known by past experience that he was too good to be true, but as you said...love will make a fool of you every time. I thought all my dreams had come true. Hal was handsome, successful, exciting, masterful. Materially, he had it all as well. The mansion on the water. The car. The yacht. He swept me right off my feet, I can tell you. Told me he adored me. It was just a matter of time, I thought, till he proposed. I was on cloud nine till I picked up the paper one day and saw his photograph on the front page.'

'Must have been one bad day.'

'That's an understatement, I can assure you. I was devastated.'

'Did you have to testify at his trial?'

'No. Which was fortunate. Also fortunate that this all happened in another state. I hadn't told my parents about Hal, you see. But I was going to, once we were engaged. I thought he'd be a pleasant surprise after all the going-nowhere men I'd been with in the past. Some surprise he'd have turned out to be!'

'Just as well he was arrested when he was, then.'

'I didn't quite see it that way at the time,' Isabel muttered.

'No. Just as I didn't see I was better off without Liz. But we're both better off without both of them, Isabel. Much better off. And you're better off without Luke, no matter what you think now. He didn't love you.'

'Love I can do without from now on.'

Rafe looked at her. 'Oh, I don't know. Love still has a certain appeal.'

'I can't see what. It makes you do things. Stupid things. Irrational things.'

'Mmm. You could be right there.' Because for the next two days he was going to do the stupidest, most irrational things in his life!

'Where on earth is that food?' Isabel said irritably.

'It'll be here soon. Meanwhile, have some more champagne,' he added, and topped up her glass. 'Good, isn't it?'

'Yes. But if I don't eat soon it'll go straight to my head. I have a very low intoxication level with champagne. It can make me tipsy quicker than anything else.'

'Is that so? Well, there's no worry in being a bit tipsy, is there? It won't make you do anything later that you wouldn't be doing anyway.'

The eyes she set upon him over the rim of her glass were very dry. 'My, aren't we full of the sauce tonight?'

I hope so, Rafe thought ruefully. Because my sauce is going to have to work very hard to do the job from now on. He didn't dare cut the whole top off every condom he used during the next two days. She might notice. He really could only risk a pin-prick or two. Except perhaps tonight...

Isabel's powers of observation could very well be limited if she got well and truly sloshed. If he was clever with what position he used, he might get away with not using anything at all.

The thought excited, then worried him.

It was a stupid thing to do, as she said. Stupid and irrational. She didn't love him. She wouldn't marry him.

At best, he would be a father to their child at a distance, having limited access.

But so what? he thought recklessly. He was still going to do it, wasn't he?

CHAPTER ELEVEN

ISABEL woke with a moan on her lips. The sun was shining in through the open doorway of the bure, indicating Rafe was already up, probably having his early-morning swim.

'That man must have a constitution of iron,' she muttered as she dragged aside the mosquito net and tried to sit up. But the room spun alarmingly and there was a bongo drummer—complete with drums—inside her head.

With a low groan, Isabel sank back carefully onto the pillows then ever so slowly rolled onto her side. The room gradually stopped spinning.

It was then that she saw the tall glass of water sitting next to the bed, alongside a foil sheet of painkillers.

'What a thoughtful thing to do,' she murmured, though not yet daring to move. In a minute she would take a couple of those pills Rafe had left her. Meanwhile, she would close her eyes and just do nothing.

Isabel closed her eyes and tried to do nothing, but her mind was by now wide awake. She began thinking about last night after dinner. In the end, they hadn't got anyone else to run them back to their jetty. Rafe had said he was fine to operate the boat and she'd been far too tipsy to worry.

Tipsy! Hardly an adequate word to describe her state of intoxication. She'd been seriously sloshed. Not Rafe though, yet he'd consumed as many glasses of wine as she had. Or had he? Perhaps not. He'd talked a lot between courses, and she'd just sat there, sipping her wine and listening to him like some fatuous female fool, thinking how gorgeous he was and how stupid Liz was to dump him.

No, Isabel finally conceded. Rafe hadn't consumed nearly as much wine as she had. If he had, he wouldn't have been able to make such beautiful love to her as he had after they'd come home.

Not that she could remember it all. Some bits were pretty hazy. But she could remember the feel of his hands on her as he undressed her and caressed her. So gentle and tender. The same with his kisses. His mouth had flowed all over her and she had dissolved from one orgasm to another.

She'd never known climaxes could be like that. Blissful and relaxing. Her bones had felt like water by the time he'd rolled her onto her side, rather like she was lying now. Only last night Rafe's naked body had been curled around her back.

Isabel's stomach contracted at the thought. That was one thing she hadn't forgotten. How he'd felt when he'd first slipped inside her. She moaned at the memory. It had felt so good. Even better when he'd begun to move.

Never had she been so lost in a man's arms, her mind and body like mush. She hadn't come again. But, Rafe must have. She had a vague recollection of his crying out. But after that, all memory ceased. She must have fallen asleep. And now here she was the next morning with a parched mouth and a vicious headache, whilst Rafe was down at the beach, no doubt bright-eyed and bushy-tailed.

A shadow fell across the corner of her eye and she rolled over just enough to see Rafe walk through the sun-drenched doorway. His dark silhouette eventually lightened to reveal that she'd been right. He had been swimming, thankfully dressed in board shorts. She couldn't cope with him in full-frontal nudity this morning.

'How's the head?' he said as he walked towards the bed.

'Awful. Many thanks for the tablets and the water.'

'My pleasure. And it *was*,' he added with a devilish grin.

'Don't be cocky. I was pretty plastered.'

'So I noticed. You know you're very agreeable when you're plastered.'

'I really couldn't say. Last night is somewhat hazy.'

'You mean you can't remember anything?'

Isabel caught an odd note in Rafe's question. Was he pleased or offended? 'I didn't say that. I said hazy, as in…hazy.'

'Ahh. Hazy. Hazy word, hazy.'

'You were pretty good, if that's what you're waiting for.'

He smiled. 'That's nice to hear.'

'Different, though.'

Rafe's stomach flipped over. 'Different?' he asked, trying not to panic. 'In what way, different?'

She shrugged. 'Gentler. Sweeter. Different.'

Rafe smiled his relief. 'Well, I didn't need to rush it. You weren't making any of your usual control-losing demands.'

Isabel was taken aback. 'What do you mean, control-losing demands?'

'Honey, you have a very impatient nature when it comes to sex. It's always faster, Rafe. Harder. Deeper. Again. More. No more. Stop. Don't stop. The list is endless.'

'That's not true!' she denied hotly.

'Perhaps a slight exaggeration on my part. But it was still a rather nice change to know I could take my time and do exactly what I wanted to do with your total co-operation. I really enjoyed it.'

And how! Rafe thought.

Any apprehension over his bold decision not to use any protection had disappeared once he'd put his plans into action. Knowing that a child could possibly result from his lovemaking had added an emotional dimension Rafe hadn't anticipated. When he'd felt his seed spilling into her he'd thought his heart would burst with elation. And when she'd gone to sleep in his arms afterwards he'd been consumed by feelings so powerful and deep that they'd revolutionised his ideas on what loving a person was all about.

Seeing Liz last night was the best thing that could have happened to him. What a fool he'd been, choosing a solitary life for fear of being hurt again. Fair enough to withdraw into his cave for a while. But it had been years, for pity's sake. Years of keeping women at a distance, except sexually, and telling himself—and everyone else—that he didn't want marriage and a family, when the truth was he'd become too much of a coward to risk his male ego a second time. He'd been afraid of being dumped again, afraid of rejection.

Not any more. He was going to take a leaf out of Isabel's book and go after what he wanted. Which was *her* as his wife as well as the mother of his child. Or children. Heck, he wasn't going to stop at just one. He'd hated being an only child.

But he couldn't tell her all that yet. He couldn't even tell her how much he loved her. She wasn't ready for such an announcement. But she would be, in time. And when Mother Nature eventually took her course.

It was to be hoped that last night had done the trick. But if it hadn't, he'd already doctored a few more condoms for today. If at first you don't succeed, Rafe, then try, try again.

Trying again had never looked so pleasurable. Pity she had a hangover. Still, that would pass.

'God, I can't stand people looking perky when I'm dying,' Isabel grumbled.

'What you need is a refreshing swim,' Rafe suggested.

She groaned. 'My head is already swimming, thank you very much. Do you think I could con you into getting me a cup of coffee?'

He jumped up off the foot of the bed. 'One steaming mug of sweet black coffee coming up!'

Isabel groaned again. Not only perky, but energetic. He even started whistling.

Still, she had to concede Rafe wasn't anything like she'd first thought. Oh, she didn't doubt he was a bit of a ladies' man. And marriage and children were not part of his life plan. But he wasn't at all arrogant, or selfish. He was actually quite considerate, and highly sensitive. That Liz female had really hurt him, stupid greedy amoral woman that she was.

His dad's death had scarred him as well. Isabel had been moved last night when Rafe had told her how his father had been a country rep for a wine company, travelling all over New South Wales, selling his products into hotels and clubs and restaurants. Rafe had been just eight when his dad's car had hit a kangaroo at night and careered off the road into a tree, killing him instantly. Unfortunately, his father hadn't been a great success as a salesman—a bit of a dreamer, though in the nicest possible way—and money had been tight for his widow and son after his demise.

But he'd been a great success as a dad. Clearly, Rafe had adored him. His voice had choked up when he'd told Isabel that the only things his father had left him in a material sense were a camera and a pair of phantom's-head cuff-links. Father and son had had a real thing for the Phantom, his Dad always bringing Rafe home a *Phantom Comic* after he'd been away. They would always read it together that night. Isabel had been moved to hear that, when one of the prized cuff-links had been lost during a house move Rafe had had the other made into an earring and never took it off for fear of losing it as well. How he must have loved that man!

It was a pity he shied away from being a father himself. With his dad's example to go by, he'd probably be a very good one.

She sighed. That was the incorrigible romantic in her talking again. Next thing she'd have him returning with her coffee and saying he'd changed his mind about what he wanted in life, after which he'd declare his undying love and beg her to marry him.

Fat chance!

'Here's your coffee, lover. Now, stop all that sighing and drink up. Oh, for pity's sake, you haven't even taken your headache tablets yet. Or drunk the water. How do you expect to feel better unless you rehydrate yourself? No, no coffee for you till you've done the right thing. And there'll be no more drinking to excess in future. It's no good for you.'

Isabel glared at him. 'And there I was, thinking you weren't the bullying bossy pain in the neck I'd first met. But I was deluding myself. The only reason you want me to feel better is so that you can have more of what you got last night.'

He grinned the cheekiest sexiest grin. 'You could be right there.'

Isabel glowered at him as she popped two tablets into her mouth and swallowed the water.

'A shower or the sea?' he said, eyeing her rather salaciously where the sheet had slipped down to her waist.

Isabel didn't have to look down to know what he was seeing. Maybe *she* wasn't too perky this morning, but her nipples still were.

And she was so wet down there it wasn't funny.

'I think a spa bath is in order,' she said. 'Alone,' she added firmly.

'I could scrub your back,' Rafe offered.

'No.'

'Spoilsport.'

'And then, after breakfast, I'd like to do something unenergetic. I noticed there was a pack of cards in the cupboard over there.'

'Cards,' he repeated drily. He hated playing cards. His mother was a fanatic at euchre and cribbage, and used to rope him in when she couldn't find another partner. She always won so there hadn't been much fun in it for him.

'There's plenty of other games in there as well, if you'd prefer,' she went on, no doubt hearing his reluctance.

Rafe eyed her with determination. The only games he aimed to play today were those of the erotic kind. He couldn't afford to waste the whole of this very critical twenty-four hours. She might be ovulating at this very second.

But then an idea came to him.

'Okay,' he agreed. 'But, to make it interesting, let's bet on the outcome of each game.'

She frowned. 'For money, you mean?'

'Don't be silly. What would be the fun in that?'

'What, then?'

'If I win, you have to do whatever I want. And vice versa.'

Her eyes widened. 'Are we talking sexual requests here?'

'Not necessarily. I might ask you to go for a swim with me. Or cook me a meal. Or give me a massage.'

Yeah, right, she thought ruefully.

'I won't agree to *anything*, Rafe, especially sexually. There has to be limitations.'

'Nothing too kinky, then. Nothing you think the other person wouldn't like.'

That was far too broad a canvas! 'I…I don't want to be tied to that hammock again.' Not in the daylight. That would be just too embarrassing for words.

'Fair enough. What would you rather be tied to?'

'Rafe!'

'Only kidding.' Hell, he didn't want to tie her up. He just wanted to make her a mother.

Isabel could feel the heat spreading all through her body. This was just the kind of thing which turned her on. Oh, he was wicked.

'Let me have that bath and some breakfast first, then,' she said, trying not to sound too eager. 'You find whatever game you think you would prefer.' And hopefully one that he was darned good at playing. Because she didn't want to win, did she? She wanted him to win.

He chose an ingenious little game called Take It Easy,

and by eleven they were sitting on the terrace, playing. The trouble was luck rather than skill played a large part and, even if you didn't try, sometimes you still won. Each game didn't last all that long and the rules suggested you play three games then totalled up the scores to see who won.

Isabel won the first round, by one point, despite not concentrating at all.

'Oh,' she said, trying not to sound disappointed by the result.

Rafe eyed her expectantly across the table. 'Well? What cruel fate awaits me, oh, mistress mine?'

'You said nothing kinky,' she reminded him.

'No, I said nothing *too* kinky.'

'You also said it didn't have to be a sexual request.' Surely she would lose next time and then she would be forced to do what *he* wanted. That would be much more fun. She would wait. 'So I'd like a toasted ham, cheese and tomato sandwich, please. And a tall glass of iced orange juice.'

'What?' he snapped, his face frustrated. 'You just had breakfast half an hour ago.'

'I'm sorry but I'm still hungry,' she said blithely.

When he just sat there, scowling at her, she crossed her arms. 'Are you welching on your bet already?'

'You'll keep, madam,' he muttered, then went to do her bidding.

Five minutes later he returned with the sandwich on a plate and a very tall glass of frosted orange juice. The fridge and freezer really were very well stocked, especially with the ingredients for easy-to-make snacks. Honeymooners and illicit lovers—who were the likely bookers of the private bures—apparently didn't surface back at the main resort for meals all that often.

Isabel accepted the toasted sandwich and ate it very slowly, pretending to savour every bite. In actual fact, she wasn't at all hungry. She just hadn't been able to think of anything else to ask for. The orange juice was nice, though, and she drank it down with deep gulps. Her hangover had long receded but she was still probably a bit dehydrated.

'Ahh,' she said, and placed the empty glass on the empty plate, pushing them both to one side. 'That was lovely, Rafe. Thank you. Shall we get on with the next round?'

'By all means.'

Rafe won. Easily.

'Oh, dear,' Isabel said.

'My turn, it seems,' Rafe said with cool satisfaction in his voice, and a smouldering look in his eyes.

Isabel began to tremble inside.

'Take off your sarong,' he commanded.

When he didn't add anything else, she just looked at him. 'That's it? Just take off my sarong?'

'Yes. Do you have a problem with that?'

She gulped. It was far less than she was expecting. And yet...

It suddenly hit her that he meant for her to sit there, playing the next round of the game, in the nude. The deviousness of his mind excited her, as did the idea.

Isabel felt her blood begin to charge around her veins as she stood up and slowly undid the knot which tied her sarong between her breasts. Their eyes met and she was just about to drop it down onto the terracotta flagstones when the phone rang.

'Leave it,' Rafe commanded thickly. 'It's probably just Reception wanting to know if we want a picnic lunch brought over.'

Isabel tried to do what he said. Tried to ignore it. But she couldn't, especially when it just kept on ringing.

'I can't,' she blurted out and, retying the sarong, she hurried in to answer it.

'Hello,' she said breathlessly.

'Isabel?'

'Rachel!'

'I'm so s…sorry to bother you,' she cried, her voice shaking.

'Rachel, what's wrong?'

'It's Lettie. She…she's gone, Isabel.'

'You mean…passed away?'

'She wandered out of the house a couple of nights back when I was asleep and got a chill. She… she wasn't wearing any clothes, you see. She often took them off. Anyway, by the time I realised she was gone and the police found her, wandering in some park, she was shivering from the cold and it quickly developed into pneumonia. Her doctor put her in hospital and pumped her full of antibiotics, and they said she was going to be all right, but last night she…she had a heart attack and they couldn't save her.'

'Oh, Rachel, I'm so sorry.'

'You know, I thought I'd be relieved if and when she died,' she choked out. 'You've no idea what it's been like. The endless days and nights. The utter misery and futility of it all. Because I knew she'd never get better. She was only going to get worse. And worse. I used to lie in bed some nights and hope she wouldn't wake up in the morning. But now that she has died, I…I'm not relieved at all. I'm devastated. I look at her empty bed and just cry and cry and cry. I…I can't function, Isabel. I needed to talk to you. That's why I had to call. I needed to hear your voice and know that somewhere in this world there was someone who loved me.' At that, she broke down and wept.

'It's all right, Rachel. I'll ring Mum and Dad straight away and get them to go and bring you home to their place. And I'll be back in Sydney as soon as I can.'

'But…but you can't,' she cried, pulling herself together. 'Your mum will know, if you do that.'

'Know what?'

'That you didn't go to Dream Island with me. She'll know you went with…with some man.'

'Oh, never mind that. What does that matter? So she'll think I'm wicked for a while. She'll get over it. Now, you hang in there, Rach, and don't go doing anything silly.'

'Such as what?' Rachel sniffled.

'Such as drinking too much of Lettie's sherry. Or sleeping with the gardener.'

'I don't have a gardener,' she said mournfully. 'But

if I did I would sleep with him, no matter what he looked like. I'm so lonely, Isabel.'

'Not for long, sweetie. Just hang in there. I'll ring Mum straight away and get her to ring you.'

'All right.'

'You are home, aren't you?'

'What? Yes, yes, I'm home.'

Isabel's heart turned over. The poor darling. She sounded shattered. 'Okay, don't go anywhere till Mum rings you.'

'Where would I go?'

'I don't know. Shopping, perhaps. Or back to the hospital.'

'I don't want to ever go near that hospital ever again.' And she started to weep again.

'Oh, Rachel, please don't cry. You'll make me cry.' Isabel's chin was already beginning to quiver.

'S…sorry,' Rachel blubbered. 'Sorry.'

Isabel swallowed. 'Don't be sorry. Don't you ever be sorry. I'll try to get a flight back today. At worst, it will be tomorrow. Meanwhile, you do just what Mum tells you to do. She'll bombard you with cups of sweet tea and plate-loads of home-made lamingtons but don't say no. You could do with fattening up a bit. Do you realise you've lost most of those fantastic boobs of yours? You know, I used to be jealous of those at school. You've no idea. But they'll bounce back. And so will you, love. Trust me on that.'

'I knew I was right to ring you,' Rachel said with a not so distressed-sounding sigh.

'If you hadn't, I'd have been very annoyed. Now, I must go. Loads to do. See you soon, sweetie. Take care.'

Isabel hung up with a weary sigh. Rachel was right about one thing. Her mother was not going to be pleased with her little deception over this holiday.

But that was just too bad. Squaring her shoulders, Isabel swept the receiver up again, and asked Reception for an outside line.

'I gather the honeymoon's over.'

Isabel spun round to find Rafe standing in the doorway.

'How much did you hear?'

'All of it.'

'Then you know I have to go home. You can stay for the rest of the fortnight if you want to.'

He stared at her as though she were mad. 'Now, why would I want to do that? Without you here with me, Isabel, it would just be a waste of time. No, I'll be coming back to Sydney with you. If you find there aren't any available seats going back this afternoon, you could have Reception offer the rest of this pre-paid jaunt to all the couples on the island whose holiday ends today. Someone is sure to take you up on it.'

'That's an excellent idea, Rafe. Thank you.'

'I am good for some things besides sex, you know.'

Isabel frowned at the slightly bitter edge in his voice. What had got into him? Did he think she was happy about having to leave?

'Look, I'm sorry, Rafe. I hardly planned this. I'd rather be staying here with you than going back home to a heartbroken friend. But fate has decided otherwise. Rachel needs me and she needs me *now*. I'm not going to let her down.'

'I appreciate that. Honest I do. I admire people who are there for their friends when they're needed. I guess that's the crux of my discontent. The fact you didn't consider I'd be there for *you* during the next few undeniably difficult days. You just dismissed me like some hired gigolo whose services were no longer required. I thought we'd moved beyond that. I thought you genuinely liked me.'

'I…I do like you. But what we've had together here… We both knew it was just a fantasy trip, Rafe. It's been fantastic but it's not real life. Come on the plane with me by all means, but once we get back to Sydney I think we should go our separate ways.'

'Do you, now?' he bit out. 'Well, I don't.'

'You don't?'

'No. As far as what we've had here… Yes, it has been fantastic, but I think we can have something better once we get back to Sydney. And we can be good friends as well.'

'But…'

'But nothing. You like me. I like you. A lot. On top of that, we are very sexually compatible. Face it, Isabel, you're not the sort of woman who's ever going to live the life of a nun. You like sex far too much. So don't look a gift-horse in the mouth. Where else are you going to find a man who's prepared to be your friend as well as your lover? A man, moreover, who knows how to turn you on just like that.' And he snapped his fingers. 'You'll go a long way before you come across that combination again.'

He was right, of course. He was ideal.

Too ideal. She was sure to fall hopelessly in love with him. Sure to. But she hadn't as yet. She could still walk away.

But then she thought of what Rachel had said about being so lonely that she'd sleep with anyone, and she knew she wouldn't be able to walk away for ever. One night, when she was alone in that town house at Turramurra, she'd pick up the phone and call Rafe and ask him to come over.

Take what he's offering you now, came the voice of temptation. And if you fall in love with him?

She would cross that bridge when she came to it.

'So you want to be my day-time friend and night-time lover, is that it?'

'No. I want to be your friend *and* lover all the time. I see no reason to relegate our sex life just to night.'

An erotic quiver rippled down her spine. She didn't stand a chance of resisting this man. Why damage her pride by trying? But that same pride insisted she keep some control over the relationship. She could do that, surely.

'You're so right, Rafe,' she said, adopting what she hoped was a suitably firm woman-in-control expression. 'Things *have* worked out between us far better than I ever imagined they would. You're exactly what I need in my life. But please don't presume that my agreeing to continue with our relationship gives you any rights to tell me how to run my life. I know you don't agree with my decision to have a baby on my own, but I aim to do just that, and nothing and no one is going to stop me!'

CHAPTER TWELVE

RAFE sat silently beside Isabel on the flight to Sydney late that afternoon, planning and plotting his next move.

He'd been furious with fate at first for interrupting them. But, in the end, things hadn't worked out too badly. Isabel had at least agreed to go on seeing him. As for her declaration that nothing and no one was going to stop her from having a baby…little did she know but he was her best ally in that quest. He hoped to have her pregnant well before she got round to doing that artificial insemination rubbish.

The captain announcing that they'd begun their descent into Sydney had Isabel turning towards him for the first time in ages.

'I'll drop you off on the way home,' she said.

'Fine. What about tomorrow?'

'What about tomorrow?'

'Will you be needing me?'

She stared at him. 'I thought you said you didn't like my treating you like some gigolo,' she said agitatedly. 'That was a rather gigolo-sounding question.'

'I meant as a friend, Isabel,' he reproved, thinking to himself he had a long way to go to get her trust. That bastard Hal had a lot to answer for.

'Oh. Sorry. I'm not used to men just wanting to be my friend.'

'I thought you said you were friends with Luke first.'

'Yes, well, Luke was the exception to the rule.'

'St Luke,' he muttered.

'Not quite, as it turned out.'

'No. So what about tomorrow?'

She sighed. 'I think I should spend tomorrow with Rachel.'

Rafe had no option but to accept her decision. Which meant if she hadn't conceived this month he'd have to wait till her next cycle before trying again.

Still, he admired Isabel for the way she'd dropped everything and raced to this Rachel's side. There weren't too many people these days who would have done that. He liked to think he was a good friend, but he suspected he'd become somewhat selfish and self-centred during his post-Liz years, another result of his bruised male ego which he wasn't proud of.

'What about the next day?' he asked.

'The funeral's then.'

'I'll take you.'

'No.'

'*Yes*. I'm not going to let you hide me away like some nasty secret, Isabel. Your mother already knows you went off to Dream Island with a man. I heard you tell her on the phone. I also gather you took quite a bit of flak about it. I didn't like that. In fact, I wanted to snatch that phone right out of your hand and tell your mother the truth.'

'The…the truth?'

'Yes. You are *not* cheap or easy, which I gather was the gist of her insults. You are one classy lady and I'm one lucky guy to be having a relationship with you. You're also a terrific friend and, I'll warrant, a terrific daughter. Someone should tell your mum that some day, and that someone just might be me.'

'That's sweet of you, Rafe, but you'd be wasting your time. Mum suffers from a double generation gap. She's still living back in the fifties and simply can't come to terms with the fact I'd go away with you like that so soon after meeting you. She was not only shocked, but ashamed.'

'Sounds like she suffers from double standards as well,' Rafe pointed out irritably. 'I'll bet she wasn't shocked when she found out your precious ex-fiancé leapt into bed with his new dolly-bird less than an hour after meeting her. And I'll bet she thought that was perfectly all right!'

'No. No, I don't think she thought that at all. It's hard for her to accept modern ways, Rafe. She's seventy years old.'

'That's no excuse.'

'No, but it's a reason. She'll calm down eventually. Meanwhile, I think it's best not to throw you in her face.'

'Isabel,' he said firmly, '*you* are *thirty* years old. Way past the age of adulthood. You say you're going to live your life as you see fit. Well that should include in front of your mother.'

'That's all very well for you to say. You don't practise what you preach. You told me you lie to your mother all the time. You even pretend you're going to get married some day when you know very well that you're not.'

'That's all in the past. I'm going to be honest with her in future.' No trouble, Rafe thought. Because he *was* going to get married now. To Isabel.

'Yeah, right. Pity I won't be there to see the new-leaf Rafe.'

You will be. Don't you worry about that.

'I'm coming with you to that funeral, Isabel. And that's that!'

Isabel glared at him. The man simply couldn't be told!

'Be it on your head then,' she snapped. 'And don't say I didn't warn you.'

By five o-clock on the day of the funeral, Rafe almost wished he'd heeded her warning. The service was over and they were back at Isabel's parents' place for the wake, and he was looking for a place to hide.

Unfortunately, there weren't too many people for Rafe to hide behind. It had been a very small funeral. Isabel and Rachel, whom Rafe had warmed to on first meeting today, had been cornered by some large woman, leaving Rafe to fend for himself.

The chill coming his way from Mrs Hunt was becoming hard to take, so were the disapproving looks at his earring. Goodness knew what would have been the woman's reaction if he hadn't shaved that morning. Or put on his one and only dark and thankfully conservatively styled suit.

Rafe valiantly ignored the dagger-like glances he was getting from his hostess as he filled his plate from the buffet set out in the lounge room. After checking that Isabel and Rachel were still occupied in the corner, he headed out to the front porch, where he'd seen a seat on the way in, and where he hoped to eat his food in peace, without having to tolerate Mrs Hunt's deadly glares.

But fate was not going to be kind. He'd barely sat down when she followed him through the front door and marched over to stand in front of him. Rafe looked up from the plate he'd just balanced on his lap, keeping his face impassive despite his instantly thudding heart.

Formidable was the word which came to mind to describe Isabel's mother. Handsome, though. She would have been a fine-looking woman when she was younger. Though she did look trapped in a time warp, her grey hair permed into very tight waves and curls, and her belted floral dress with its pleated skirt reflecting a bygone era.

'Mr Saint Vincent...' she began, then hesitated, not because she didn't know what she was going to say, Rafe reckoned, but because she wanted to make him feel uncomfortable.

Her strategy worked. But be damned if he was going to let it show.

'Yes, Mrs Hunt?' he returned coolly, picking up a sandwich from the plate and taking a bite.

'Might I have a little word with you in private?'

He shrugged. 'We're perfectly alone here, so feel free to go for it.'

Her top lip curled. 'That's rather the catch cry of your generation, isn't it?' she sneered. 'Feeling free to go for whatever you want.'

'Good, isn't it? Better than being all uptight and hypocritical, like your generation.'

'How dare you?' she exclaimed, her cheeks looking as if they'd been dabbed with rouge.

'How dare *you*, Mrs Hunt? I am a guest in your home. Are you always this rude to your guests?'

'I have every right to be rude to a man who's taking wicked advantage of my daughter.'

'You think that's what I'm doing?'

'I know that's what you're doing. Isabel would never normally go off like that with some man she'd only just met. You knew she was on the rebound. But that didn't stop you, did it?'

Rafe decided to nip this in the bud once and for all. He figured he had nothing to lose, anyway. 'No,' he agreed, putting his plate down on the seat beside him and standing up, brushing his hands of crumbs as he did so. 'No, it didn't stop me, Mrs Hunt. And I'll tell you why. Because I'm in love with your daughter. I have been ever since the first moment we met. I love her and I want to marry her.'

The woman's eyes almost popped out of her head.

'Of course, I haven't told her this yet,' he went on. 'She's not ready for it. She won't be ready for it for a while, because at this moment her trust in the male sex is so low that she simply won't believe me. She, like you, thinks I'm only with her for the sex. Which is not true.'

'You mean you're…you're *not* sleeping with her?'

Rafe had to smile. 'Now, ma'am, let's not get our wires crossed here. I didn't say that. I *am* a man, not a eunuch. And your daughter is *very* beautiful. But Isabel has much more to offer a man than just sex. She's one very special lady with a special brand of pride and courage. It's a shame her own mother doesn't recognise that fact.'

'But I *do*! Why, I think she's just wonderful.'

'Funny. I get the impression you haven't told her that too often. Or at all. I gather she thinks you think she's some kind of slut.'

'I do not think anything of the kind! The very idea!'

'Well, she must have got that idea from somewhere. Get with it, Mrs Hunt, or you just might lose your daughter altogether. She's a woman of independent means now and doesn't need you to put a roof over her head. She doesn't need your constant criticisms and disapproval either.'

'But… But… Oh, dear, me and my big mouth again…'

She looked so stricken that Rafe was moved to some sympathy for her. Perhaps he'd been a bit harsh. But someone had to stand up for Isabel. None of the men in her past had, least of all St bloody Luke!

'She needs you to love her unconditionally,' he went on more gently. 'Not just when she's doing what *you* think is right. Because what you think is right, Mrs Hunt, just might be wrong. And please…don't tell her what I said about being in love with her. If you do, you'll ruin everything.'

'You really love her?'

'More than I would ever have thought possible. I'm going to marry your daughter, Mrs Hunt. It's only a question of time.'

Her joy blinded him. 'Oh. Oh, that's wonderful news. I've been so worried for her. All her life, all she's ever wanted was to get married and…and… Oh, dear…' She broke off and gnawed at her bottom lip for a few seconds, worrying the life out of Rafe. What now?

'You do know Isabel wants a baby very badly, don't you?' she finally went on. 'That won't be a problem, will it? I know a lot of men these days aren't so keen on having children.'

Rafe smiled his relief. 'Not a problem at all, Mrs Hunt. Hopefully, it's the solution.'

'The solution?' She looked mystified for a moment. But then the clouds cleared from her astute grey eyes. 'Oh,' she said, nodding and smiling. 'Oh, I see.'

'I trust Isabel will have your full approval and support if I'm successful in my plan? You won't start judging and throwing verbal stones again.'

'You can depend on me, Rafe.'

'That's great, Mrs Hunt.'

'Dot. Call me Dot.'

'Dot.' He grinned at her. 'Wish me luck, Dot.'

'You won't need too much luck, you sexy devil.'

'Dot! I'm shocked.'

'I'm not too old that I can't see what Isabel sees in you. But I'm not so sure that not telling her you love her is the right tactic.'

'Trust me, Dot. It is.'

'If you say so. Heavens, I have to confess you've surprised me. Look, I'd better go inside or Isabel might come out and catch us together, and she might start asking awkward questions. She thinks I don't like you.'

'Gee. I wonder what gave her that idea?'

Dot's fine grey eyes sparkled with a mixture of guilt and good humour. 'You are a cheeky young man too, aren't you?'

'Go lightly on the young, Dot. I'm over thirty.'

She laughed. 'That's young to me. But I take your point and I'll try to get with it, as you said.'

Dot was not long gone and Rafe had just sat down again to finish his food when Isabel burst out onto the porch. 'I've been looking for you. Mum said you were out here. What on earth did you say to her just now?'

'Nothing much.' Rafe hoped his face was a lot calmer than his insides. The more time he spent with Isabel the more hopelessly in love with her he was. And the more desperate for all his plans to succeed. 'Why?'

'Well, she actually smiled at me and told me how much she liked you. You could have knocked me over with a feather. She's been giving you killer looks all day, then suddenly she *likes* you? You must have said something.'

'I told her she had a wonderful daughter and I was going to marry you.'

Isabel blinked, stared, then burst out laughing. 'You *didn't*!'

'I did, indeed.'

'Oh, Rafe, you're wicked. First you lie to your mother about getting married, and now to mine. Still, it worked.'

Rafe almost told her then. Told her it wasn't a lie, that he was crazy about her and did want to marry her. But it simply was too premature for such declarations.

'How's Rachel coping?' he asked, deftly changing the subject.

'Not too bad, actually. Did you see that woman we were talking to?'

'The one built like a battleship?'

'That's the one. Her name's Alice McCarthy and Rachel does alterations for her. Did I tell you that's how Rachel's been making some money at home?'

'Yes, I think you did mention it.'

'She's a darned good dressmaker, too, but alterations pay better and take less time. Anyway, Alice has this son. His name's Justin.'

'Oh, no, not another match-making mother. Poor Rachel. She's deep in grief and some old battleaxe is already lining her up for her son.'

'Oh, do stop being paranoid. And Alice is not a battle-axe. She's very sweet. Anyway, this Justin doesn't want a wife. He wants a secretary. As for Rachel being in grief, she needs to get out and about as quickly as possible, otherwise she'll get even more lonely and depressed than she already is. A job is ideal. She'll have to interview, of course, but Alice is going to twist her son's arm to at least give her a go for a while.'

'That's nice of her, but can Rachel do the job? Has she ever been a secretary before?'

'Has she ever been a secretary before!' Isabel scoffed. 'I'll have you know that Rachel was a finalist in the Secretary of the Year award one year. Of course, that was a few years ago, and she has lost a bit of confidence since then, but nothing which can't be put to right with some boosting up from her friends.'

'Mmm. Tell me about this Alice's son. What does he do for a crust?'

'He's some high-flying executive in the city. One of those companies with fingers in lots of pies. Insurance. Property development. You know the kind of thing.'

'What happened to his present secretary? He must have one.'

'The story goes that she suddenly resigned last month. Flew over to England a few weeks back for her niece's wedding, realised how homesick she was for her mother country, came back just to get her things, and quit. He's been making do with a temp but he's not thrilled. Says she's far too flashy-looking and far too flirtatious. He can't concentrate on his work.'

'My heart goes out to him,' Rafe said drily. 'Still, I guess his wife might not be pleased.'

'He's divorced.'

'What's his problem, then?'

Isabel sighed. She should have known a man like Rafe

wouldn't see a problem. If he was in the same position, he'd just have the girl on his desk every lunchtime and not think twice about it.

'Office romances are never a good idea, Rafe,' she tried explaining. 'This is something you might not appreciate, since you don't work in a traditional office. *And* since you're not female. If a female employee has an affair with a male colleague, especially her boss, it's always the girl who ends up getting the rough end of the pineapple.'

He laughed. 'What a delicate way of putting it.'

Isabel rolled her eyes with utter exasperation. 'Truly. Must you always put a sexual connotation on everything?'

'Honey, I'm not the one putting a sexual connotation on this. This divorced bloke thinks his sexy temp has the hots for him and he doesn't like it. Rather makes you wonder why. Is he mentally deranged? Otherwise involved? Gay? Or just bitter and twisted?'

'Maybe he's the kind of man who doesn't like mixing business with pleasure. Unlike *some* men we know.'

'Man's a fool. He's got it made by the sound of it. Still, Rachel should suit him. She's hardly what you'd call flashy. *Or* flirtatious.' More like shy and retiring. Sweet, though. Rafe really liked her.

'No, not at the moment. But she used to be very outgoing. And drop-dead gorgeous.'

'Mmm. Hard to visualise.' The Rachel he'd met today had been a long way from drop-dead gorgeous. Okay, so there were some lingering remnants of past beauty in her thin face and gaunt body. Her eyes certainly had something.

But the hardships of minding a loved one with Alzheimer's twenty-four hours a day for over four years had clearly taken its toll. Isabel had told him Rachel was only thirty-one. But she looked forty if she was a day.

'She just needs some tender loving care,' Isabel said.

'And a serious makeover,' Rafe added. 'New hair colour. Clothes. Make-up.'

'Don't be ridiculous, Rafe. Haven't you been listening? This man doesn't want a glamour-puss for a secretary. He wants a woman who looks sensible and who doesn't turn him on.'

'Oh, yeah, I forgot. Better get her a pair of glasses then, because she has got nice eyes.'

'Yes, she does, doesn't she?'

'And get her to put on a few pounds. That anorexic look she's sporting is considered pretty desirable nowadays.'

'Are you being sarcastic?'

'Not at all. Oh, and tell her to wear black for the interview. It looks bloody awful on her. Unlike you, my darling,' he whispered in her ear, 'who looks so sexy in black that it's criminal.'

'Stop that,' Isabel choked out, shivering when he began to blow softly in her ear.

But she didn't really want him to stop. It felt like an eon since they'd been alone together, since he'd held her in his arms. She was going to go mad if she wasn't with him soon.

'Stay with me tonight,' he murmured.

'I...I can't,' she groaned. 'I'm taking Rachel home to Turramurra with me for a few days. I don't want to leave her alone just yet.'

'When, then?'

'I don't know. I'll give you a call.'

Rafe didn't want to press. But he wanted her so much. He *needed* her. And it had nothing to do with getting her pregnant.

Being in love, he decided, was hell, especially if the person you loved didn't love you back.

And she didn't. Not yet. No use pretending she did.

It was a depressing thought. The confidence which Rafe had projected to Isabel's mother suddenly seemed like so much hot air. What if she never fell in love with him? What if she never fell pregnant to him?

Then he would have nothing.

She had to fall pregnant. *Had* to. Which meant that he had to do absolutely nothing to frighten her off. He had to keep her wanting him. Had to keep her sexually intrigued.

'How about a couple of hours, then?' he suggested boldly. 'After Rachel's gone to bed. I'll pick you up and we'll go somewhere local for a nightcap, then I'll find a private place for us to park.'

Isabel was startled. '*Park*?'

'Neck, then.'

'I haven't necked in a car since I was a teenager.'

He grinned. 'Neither have I.'

'Your car has buckets seats.'

'It has a big back seat.'

She stared at him, her heart hammering inside her chest.

'Well, Isabel, what do you say?'

What did she say?

What she would always say to him.

'Make sure you bring protection with you.'

CHAPTER THIRTEEN

As RAFE turned down Isabel's street in Turramurra he glanced at the clock on the dash. Just after seven. It had taken him over an hour to drive through the rush-hour traffic from the airport to Turramurra.

Rush-hour traffic through the city was the pits at the best of times, and he wouldn't normally venture outside his front door, let alone catch a flight which landed at Mascot, anywhere near the evening peak. Unless there was a dire emergency.

In Rafe's eyes, there had been more than a dire emergency. It had been a case of life and death.

Two weeks had passed since the funeral, and almost a week since he'd seen Isabel, work having taken him to Melbourne for some magazine shoots this past week.

He'd rung her, of course. Every evening.

She'd been very chuffed on the night after Rachel got the job with Justin McCarthy. Rafe had been subjected to an hour of girl-talk stuff. Not that he'd minded. He loved hearing Isabel happy.

The next night she'd been even more excited. The two girls had spent the day shopping for a new work wardrobe for Rachel. All non-flashy, non-flirtatious clothes, Rafe had been assured. He'd received a dollar-by-dollar description of everything they'd bought.

The night after that, she'd raved on about how she was now helping Rachel clear out and clean up Lettie's house. Rachel was going to sell it, then buy a unit closer to the city. Isabel was going to look around for one for her, since she wasn't working and wasn't going to get herself another job for a while, if ever.

The following evening, however, she had been very subdued. When Rafe had asked her what was wrong she'd been evasive, saying in the end that she was just tired. But Rafe believed he knew what was bothering her. Her period—that event she could always set her clock by—hadn't arrived as expected that day.

He'd contained his own secret elation at being successful so soon, and had rung her again today from Tullamarine Airport just before he'd caught an earlier plane than he'd been intending. His original booking had been for a later flight, but he was anxious to get back to Isabel.

She'd been even more distracted during this phone-call, and when he'd said he was coming over as soon as he'd landed she'd fobbed him off, saying she was cooking dinner for her parents that night and to give her a call on the weekend.

Rafe suspected she'd come up with another excuse not to see him then as well. Which was why he'd decided to just show up on her doorstep.

The lights on in her town house told him she'd lied about going to her parents, and that really worried him.

What on earth was going through her mind? Had she

realised she didn't want a baby so badly after all? Or was it just *his* baby she didn't want?

Rafe hoped it wasn't anything like that. He hoped she was just a little shocked, and perhaps worried over what to do where he was concerned. Perhaps she'd decided not to tell him. Naturally, she'd think the pregnancy was an accident on his part and not deliberate. Perhaps she was worried he wouldn't want the child. He stupidly hadn't thought of that. Perhaps she was going to break it off with him and have his baby on her own, as she'd always planned to do.

He didn't want to entertain that other awful worry that she might get rid of his baby. Surely Isabel wouldn't do that. Even if she was late, and thought she was pregnant, she couldn't be sure yet. Even the most regular women were sometimes late.

But she wasn't late, Rafe believed as he sat there, mulling everything over. She was pregnant with his child. That was why she was acting out of character.

The time had come for a confession.

A wave of nausea claimed his stomach as he alighted from his car. Rafe hadn't felt this nervous in years, in fact, he'd *never* felt this nervous. This was worse than having his photographs exhibited, or judged. This was *him* about to be judged. Rafe, the man.

What if Isabel found him wanting in the role as father of her child? What if she didn't think him worthy? What then?

Rafe had no idea. He'd just have to take this one step at a time.

* * *

Isabel couldn't settle to anything. She wandered out into the kitchen and started making herself a cup of coffee. Not because she really wanted one but just to do something.

She *couldn't* be pregnant, she began thinking for the umpteenth time as she waited for the water to boil. Rafe had religiously used protection.

But condoms *weren't* one hundred per cent safe, came the niggling thought. Nothing was one hundred per cent safe except abstinence. And they certainly hadn't abstained during the few days they'd spent together on Dream Island. It had been full-on sex all the time. Mind-blowing, multi-orgasm sex. The kind of sex which might cause a condom to spring a little leak.

And a little leak was all that it took. Isabel recalled seeing a documentary once where just a drop of sperm had millions of eggs in it. Millions of very active eggs with the capacity to impregnate lots of women, if the timing was right.

And the timing had been pretty right, hadn't it? Perhaps not optimum time, she conceded. That had been from the Thursday till the Saturday. But they'd had sex late on the Wednesday night and that could easily have done the trick. Sperm could live for forty-eight hours, that same documentary had proudly proclaimed. Surviving half a miserable day was a cinch.

Oh, dear…

Her front doorbell ringing had Isabel spilling coffee beans all over the grey granite-topped bench. It wasn't

Rachel calling round. Isabel had not long got off the phone to Rachel, who'd told her not to be silly, she was only a day and a half late, she probably wasn't pregnant at all. Rachel had sensibly suggested buying a home-pregnancy test in the morning and putting her mind at rest.

But Isabel already knew what the result would be. She was pregnant with Rafe's child. She just knew it.

The doorbell rang a second time with Isabel still standing there, her mind still whirling.

It wasn't her parents. Tonight was raffle night down at their club. Nothing short of her giving birth would drag her mother away from that raffle.

Which event was a little way off yet.

Unlikely to be any of her new neighbours—whose names she didn't even know—wanting a cup of sugar. People rarely did that kind of the thing in the city.

No, it was Rafe. She'd heard the puzzled note in his voice when she'd put him off from coming round. But she simply hadn't been in a fit state to face him.

The fear had first begun yesterday, within hours of her not getting her period around noon, as usual. By this afternoon she'd been in a right royal flap.

Already, she could see it all. Rafe not wanting this child. Rafe making her feel terrible about her decision to have it. Rafe perhaps trying to talk her into a termination.

No, no, she could not stand that. He was the one she had to get rid of, not the baby.

The ringing changed to a loud knocking, followed by

Rafe's voice through the door. 'I know you're in there, Isabel, so please open up. I'm not going away till I speak to you.'

Isabel valiantly pulled herself together. Now's your opportunity, she lectured herself as she marched towards the front door. He already knows you lied to him about tonight. He'll be wondering why. The timing is perfect to tell him you don't want to see him any more. That this relationship—despite the great sex—isn't working for you.

Rafe knew, the moment she opened the door, that he was in trouble. She had that look in her eyes, a combination of steel and ice. He'd seen it before, the day they'd first met at his place.

'Come in,' she said curtly. 'Please excuse my appearance. I wasn't expecting any visitors tonight.'

She was wearing a simple black tracksuit and white joggers. Her hair was down and her face was free of make-up. Rafe thought she looked even more lovely than usual.

'I was just making coffee.' She turned her back on him and headed across the cream-tiled foyer towards the archway which led into the living room. 'Would you like a cup?' she threw over her shoulder.

Rafe decided to circumvent any social niceties and go straight to the heart of the matter.

'No,' he said firmly as he shut the door behind him and followed her into the stylishly furnished living room. 'I didn't come here for coffee.'

She watched him walk over to one of the cream

leather armchairs. He had a sexy walk, did Rafe. Actually, he had a sexy way of doing most things. Once settled, he glanced back up at her, his dark eyes raking her up and down, reminding Isabel that she was braless underneath her top.

Feeling her nipples automatically harden annoyed her, self-disgust giving her the courage to do what she had to do. 'If you came for sex, Rafe,' she said as she crossed her arms, 'then you're out of luck. There won't be any more sex. In fact, there won't be any more us. Period.'

'Mmm. Was that a Freudian slip, Isabel?'

Her resolve cracked a little. 'What...what do you mean?'

'I mean that's the problem, isn't it? You haven't got your period.'

She literally gaped at him, her crossed arms unfolding to dangle in limp shock at her sides.

Rafe sucked in sharply. Bingo! He was right. She was pregnant.

Suddenly, he was no longer afraid. He felt nothing but joy and pride, and love. Isabel didn't know it yet but he was going to make a great father. And a great husband, if she'd let him.

'I understand your reaction,' he said carefully. 'But you have no reason to worry. I'm here to tell you that if you are pregnant, then I will support you and the child in every way.'

She still didn't say a word.

'You *are* late, aren't you?' he probed softly.

She blinked, then shook her head as though trying to

clear the wool from her brain. 'I don't understand any of this,' she said, her hands lifting agitatedly, first to touch her hair and then to rest over her heart. 'Why would you even *think* I was pregnant?'

'I have a confession to make. There was this one occasion on Dream Island when the condom failed.'

Isabel gasped. 'Oh, that's what I thought must have happened. But why didn't you tell me?'

'I didn't want to worry you. It was too late to do anything after the event, other than get you to a doctor for the morning-after pill. And I didn't think you'd want to do that. Was I wrong, Isabel? Would you have taken that option?'

He could see by the expression in her eyes that she wouldn't have even considered it.

'I thought as much,' he said.

She almost staggered over to perch on the cream leather sofa adjacent to him. 'When…when did this happen?'

'On the Wednesday.'

She frowned. 'That night after dinner?'

'No, earlier on in the day.'

Her frown deepened. 'So all those questions you asked about my plans to get pregnant on my honeymoon… You were trying to find out what the likelihood was of my getting pregnant that day?'

'Yes,' he admitted.

'You had to have been worried.'

'No. Actually, I wasn't.'

'But that's insane! You yourself told me you never wanted to become a father.'

'Oddly enough, once it became a distinct possibility, I found I was taken with the idea.'

'*Taken* with the idea?' she exclaimed, stunned at first, then angry. 'Oh, isn't that just like a man? *Taken* with the idea. A baby's not just a fad, Rafe. It's a reality. A forever reality. A forever responsibility.'

'You think I don't know that?' he countered, his own temper rising. 'I've had longer than you to get acquainted with the reality and the responsibility entailed in my being the father of your baby, and I still like the idea. If you must know, when it seemed like a pregnancy might only be a fifty-fifty possibility, I made a conscious decision to up the odds in favour of your conceiving.'

The words were not out of his mouth more than a split second before Rafe recognised his mistake. Isabel was having enough trouble coming to terms with her 'accidental' pregnancy without his confessing to such an action. His desire to reassure her that he really did want her child could very well rebound on him. All of a sudden what he'd always considered a rather romantic decision that Wednesday night on Dream Island began developing various shades of grey about it.

'What did you do?' she demanded to know, her eyes widening.

His guilty face must have been very revealing.

'Rafe, you *didn't*!'

'Well, I...I...'

'You *did*! You had sex with me without using anything. And you deliberately got me drunk so that I wouldn't notice.'

'Well, I...I...' He'd turned into a bumbling idiot!

'How dare you do something like that without my permission? How dare you think you had that right? What kind of man are you?' She jumped to her feet, her hands finding her hips as she glared down at him.

Her ongoing outrage finally galvanised his brain, and his tongue. 'A man who's madly in love with you!' he roared back, propelling himself to his feet also. 'And I'd do it all over again. In fact, I *intended* to do it all over again, as often as I could get away with it. I even doctored a whole lot of condoms in readiness!'

Her eyes became great blue pools.

'I couldn't bear the thought of the woman I loved artificially inseminating her body with some stranger's child, when I wanted to give her *my* child. I was prepared to do anything, break every rule and cross every line, to do just that, and I don't mind admitting it. I love you, Isabel,' he claimed, grasping her shoulders, 'and I think you love me, only you're too scared to admit it, and you're too scared to trust me.

'But you shouldn't be,' he pleaded, his hands curling even more firmly over her shoulders. 'I'm nothing like the other losers you've been involved with. A fool, maybe, up till now. But a fool no longer. Seeing Liz again on that island cured me of my foolishness by making me see I was heading for the same kind of future she's ended up with. Empty and shallow, without really loving anyone or being loved in return. I took one look at you that night and thought, *This* is what I want. This woman, as my wife and the mother of my children. I love you, Isabel. Tell me you love me, too.'

Isabel searched his face, her own a tortured maze of mixed emotions. Shock. Confusion. Anguish. Maybe a measure of desperate hope in there somewhere.

'Love is more than sex, Rafe.'

'I know that.'

'Do you? Do I? Sometimes the lines between lust and love can be very blurred. I've thought myself in love so many times before, and all I've ended up with is a broken heart. And broken dreams.'

'I can understand your fear. I used to be afraid of love, too. But life without love is no life at all. Even your stupid bloody Luke found that out. Look, just tell me if you *think* you're in love with me.'

She moaned her distress at having to admit such a thing.

'All right,' Rafe said. 'You don't have to say it. I'll say it for both of us. We love each other. We've loved each other from the start. That's the truth of it and I won't let you deny it. But I also won't ask you to marry me. Not yet, anyway. All I'm asking is that you let me be a part of your life, and our baby's life, on a permanent basis.'

Isabel could hardly think. Everything was going way too fast for her. 'I...we...we don't know if there is a baby yet. Not for sure, anyway.'

'Then let's find out. Go see a doctor. We'll find one

of those twenty-four hour-surgeries. There has to be one open somewhere around here.'

'There's no need to do that. All we need is a chemist. And they're open till nine tonight.'

'Let's go, then.'

Rafe could feel the tension in her growing during the time it took to drive to a local mall, buy a pregnancy testing kit, then return. They read the instructions together, then Isabel retired to the bathroom to do what had to be done. In a couple of minutes she would confirm what he already knew. She was expecting his child.

Rafe waited patiently for the first few minutes, but when she hadn't come back downstairs after ten he marched halfway up the stairs and called out.

'Isabel? What's taking so long?'

She eventually appeared at the top of the stairs, pale-faced.

Rafe melted with love and concern for her obvious distress. 'Oh, darling, there's no need to be upset. A baby is what you wanted most in the world after all.'

'There's no baby,' she choked out. 'The test was negative.' And she burst into tears.

CHAPTER FOURTEEN

'OH, RAFE,' she sobbed, the tears spilling over and streaming down her face.

Rafe brushed aside his own disappointment to leap up the remaining steps which separated them and pull her into his arms.

'It's all right, darling,' he murmured as he pressed her shaking body to his. 'We'll make a baby for you next month. You'll see. There, there, sweetheart, don't cry so. You know what they say. If at first you don't succeed, try, try again.'

But nothing he could say would console her. She wept on and on, as though her very soul was shattered. In the end he didn't believe her pain was just because the test was negative. He believed it was caused by the build-up of all the disappointments in her life so far, culminating in this last most distressing disappointment.

When she virtually collapsed in his arms, he picked her up and carried her to bed. He didn't bother to undress her, just pulled back the covers and tipped her gently onto the mattress. Though he did yank off her joggers before covering her up with the quilt.

'Don't leave me,' she cried as he tucked her in.

'I won't,' he promised. 'I'll just go make you a hot drink.'

'No, no, I don't want a drink. I just want you. Hold me, Rafe. I feel safe when you hold me.'

He sighed at the thought. How could he stop at just holding her? Yet, at the same time, how could he refuse her? She needed him. Not as a lover, but as a friend.

Kicking off his own shoes, he climbed in beside her with the rest of his clothes on, hoping that would help. And it did. For a while. But, in the end, neither of them was content with such a platonic embrace. Yet it was Isabel who started the touching and the undressing, Isabel who decided she needed him as women had been needing the men they loved since the Garden of Eden.

Rafe could not resist her overtures and, strangely, their lovemaking turned out totally different from anything they'd shared before. It was truly *love*making. Soft. Slow. And so sweet.

Nothing but the simplest of foreplay, just face-stroking and the most innocent of kisses. Rafe's hands were gentle on her breasts and hers caressing on his back. And when the yearning to become one over-whelmed them both they merely fused together, Rafe on top, Isabel gazing adoringly up at him. They took a long time in coming, but when they did it was with such feeling, waves of rapturous pleasure rippling through their bodies, bringing with them the most amazing peace and contentment.

'I do love you,' she murmured as she lay in his arms afterwards.

Rafe sighed and stroked her hair. 'Good.'

'And I will marry you,' she added. 'If you still want me to.'

'Even better.'

'But I don't want to wait till we're married before we try again for a baby. Can we try again next month, like you said?'

'I'm putty in your hands, Isabel.'

When she hugged him even more tightly, Rafe was startled to feel tears pricking at his eyes. But that was how much he loved her, and how much her loving him meant to him. At that moment, his cup indeed runneth over.

He lay thinking about their future for a long time after she was fast asleep.

'I want you to come to lunch with my mother tomorrow,' he told her the following morning over breakfast.

Isabel pushed her hair out of her face as she glanced up at him. 'Oh, dear. Do you think she'll like me?'

'She's going to adore you.'

'You really think so? Mothers worry me a bit. She's had you all to herself all these years. I'll bet you're the apple of her eye.'

Rafe had to laugh. His mother had always found him a very difficult child. And an even more difficult teenager. He'd been one-eyed and extremely focused, determined to be a famous photographer, and even more determined never to be poor, as they'd been for many years after his father had died. At sixteen, he'd used money he'd saved from various after-school jobs to convert their single garage into a darkroom, consigning his mother's car to the street.

She'd been thrilled when he'd finally moved out of home. He believed the only reason she was fanatical about his getting married was because she was paranoid that one day fate would step in and he'd have to come home for some reason.

'Trust me, Isabel,' he said. 'My mother is not one of those mothers. She has her own life, with her own friends, pleasures and pastimes. She just wants me settled and safely married because she doesn't want to worry about me any more. Of course, she would love a grandchild or two. I won't deny that. By the way, any sign of that missing period yet?'

'No. I can't imagine where it is. I'm never late.'

'You don't think that test could have been wrong, do you?'

Isabel's stomach fluttered. She hadn't thought of that. 'I...I'm sure I followed the instructions correctly.'

'Yes, but you're not all that late yet. How far along do you have to be for it to be a reliable test?'

'It's supposed to work from two weeks.'

'Yes, but you would have only been two weeks and a day at best yesterday, Isabel. That's borderline. Perhaps we should buy another test and try again in a couple of days' time.'

Isabel recoiled at the idea. She didn't want to build up her hopes only to have them dashed again. Her emotions had been such a mess last night after Rafe arrived and made all his most amazing confessions. She'd swung from distress to delight to despair, all in the space of an hour.

She hadn't cried like that ever in her life, not even when she'd found out Hal had been a drug-dealer. Still, crying her heart out in Rafe's arms had been a deeply cleansing experience, and their lovemaking later had filled her with such hope and joy for the future that she didn't need to be pregnant now to make her happy. She was already happy just being with Rafe and knowing that he really loved her. They'd have a baby eventually. It had been silly of her to be so disappointed. And it would be silly to torture herself with another test. Better to just calmly wait for her period to arrive, then make plans for trying again during her next cycle.

'No,' she said. 'I don't want to do that. I'm sure my period is going to arrive any minute now, provided I don't start stressing about it. I think that's the problem with it. Stress.'

'I think you could be right. From now on, you are going to be relaxed and happy.'

'Sounds wonderful. So what are we going to do today?'

'I'm going to take you shopping for an engagement ring. That way, at lunch tomorrow, Mum will know I'm deadly serious about marrying you. Though it's going to cost me a pretty penny to top that rock you're still sporting on your left hand and which I presume Luke gave you.'

Isabel frowned. 'You're not jealous of Luke, are you, Rafe?'

'Well…'

'There's no need to be. I didn't love him.'

'Maybe, but you do have a lot of reminders of him around you. That ring, for starters. And this place. I don't mind the money he gave you but do you have to live in his house?'

'This was never really Luke's house. I mean, nothing in it reflects him on a personal basis. He bought it already furnished. And he wasn't living here all that long. Still, I'm quite happy to move in with *you*, Rafe, if you like. Though a terrace is not really suitable for a family. What say we sell both places and buy another one? Together.'

'Done.' Rafe smiled his satisfaction at that idea. 'Now, let's get dressed and go into the city for some serious ring-shopping.'

'Are you sure you can afford this?' Isabel asked Rafe later that morning, after she'd selected a gorgeous but expensive-looking diamond and emerald ring.

'No trouble. I'll just go ring my bank manager for a second mortgage.'

Isabel looked at him with alarm. 'I don't mind getting something cheaper.'

Rafe smiled and kissed her. 'Don't be silly. I was only joking. I can easily afford this ring, Isabel. I might not be a multi-millionaire but I have more than enough to support a wife and family. I am a very successful photographer and an astute investor, even if I say so myself.

I'll tell your dad that when I officially ask for your hand in marriage tonight.'

'When you *what*?'

'As you once pointed out to me, Isabel, your parents come from a different generation. I want to get off on the right foot with your father as well as your mother.'

'You'll get off on the right foot with my mother by just marrying me,' Isabel said drily.

Rafe smiled. 'That's what I gathered when I told her I was going to do just that at the funeral a couple of weeks back.'

Isabel was astonished, then amused. 'So that's what you did to make her like you! You are a mischievous and manipulative devil, Rafe Saint Vincent. But I love you all the same.'

'You'd want to after costing me this much money.'

'Don't worry,' she murmured, reaching up to kiss his cheek. 'If you ever run out, I have plenty.'

'Huh. Now I'm not so sure I like Luke giving you all that money, either. A man likes to be his family's provider, you know. He likes to be needed for more than just his body.'

Isabel giggled and Rafe bristled. 'What's so funny?'

'You are, going all primal male on me. Who would have believed it from the man who let me buy his body to do with as I willed for a whole fortnight?'

'I did not!'

'Oh, yes, you did. You didn't pay for a single thing on that jaunt to Dream Island.'

'I did so, too.'

'Name one.'

'I paid for the condoms.'

'Only half.'

'The three dozen I bought should have been more than enough. How was I to know I was going way with a raving nymphomaniac?'

They both realised all of a sudden that everyone in the jewellery shop had stopped what they were doing and were listening to their highly provocative bickering.

Isabel blushed fiercely whilst Rafe laughed.

'How embarrassing!' Isabel cried once they'd paid for the ring and fled outside. 'Lord knows what they thought of us.'

'Probably that you're a rich bitch and I'm your gigolo lover.'

Rafe loved it when she looked so mortified. She was such a delightful contradiction when it came to sex. So wildly uninhibited behind closed doors, but so easily embarrassed in public. Being with her was like being with a virgin and a vamp at the same time. It was a tantalising combination and one which he aimed to enjoy for the rest of their lives.

'Let's get right away from here,' Isabel urged, grabbing his arm, 'before someone comes out of that shop.'

Rafe found himself being dragged forcibly down the street. 'That's better,' she said, stopping at last. 'Oh look, Rafe, a chemist. I think I will buy another of those tests.'

'I thought you said you didn't want to.'

'I know but I…I've changed my mind.'

'Oh. Why's that?'

'Well, just now I felt kind of funny in my breasts.'

'What do you mean? Kind of funny?'

'All tingly and tight around the nipples.'

He gave her an amused glance. 'There are other explanations for that besides pregnancy, sweetness. You were just embarrassed by what happened in that shop. You find embarrassment a turn-on.'

'I do not!' She was taken aback by such an idea, and even more embarrassed.

'Yes, you do. But let's not fight about it in public. We'll pop in and buy another test, then go home. My place this time.' Thinking about her being turned on had turned *Rafe* on. He couldn't wait to get her behind closed doors again. He had a mind to photograph her as well. Afterwards. She always looked incredible afterwards. Relaxed and dreamy. He'd been wanting to capture that look with his camera for a long time. Not a nude shot. Just her face.

But she dashed upstairs for the bathroom as soon as they arrived back at his place, taking that damned test with her. A disgruntled Rafe collected his favourite camera from the darkroom, but he already knew he was wasting his time. Her mood would change once the test came back negative again. He'd been foolish to suggest the first one might have been wrong. It had just seemed logical at the time. Now he wished he'd never opened his big mouth.

Once again, she was gone ages. Lord, he hoped she wasn't up there crying again. Eventually he trudged up the stairs, not even bothering with the camera. He knew when he was beaten.

'Isabel,' he said wearily as he knocked on the bathroom door, 'please let's not go through all this again.'

The door opened and there she stood, and, yes, she was crying again, though not noisily. The tears were just running silently down her lovely cheeks.

'I should never have let you buy that bloody thing,' he muttered, hating to see her in such distress. 'Isabel, there's no need to get all upset again.'

Her smile startled him. So did the sudden sparkle in her soggy eyes

'You don't understand, darling,' she said. 'I'm not upset. I'm crying with happiness. The test was positive, Rafe. We're pregnant!'

Rafe was to wonder later in his life exactly what he felt at that moment. Time and distance did fog the memory. But it had to go down as one of the great moments in his life. He'd put it on a par with their wedding day, just over a month later, even if he had been forced to tolerate Les taking a zillion photographs and both mothers hugging and kissing him all the time.

Nothing, however, would ever eclipse the magic moment when his firstborn entered the world.

Rafe would never forget the look in Isabel's eyes as she cradled her son to her breast, then looked up at him and said, 'I'd like to call him Michael, Rafe. After your father.'

Oh, yes, that was the moment he would remember above all others.

Perhaps because he was weeping at the time.

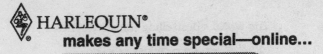

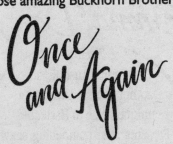

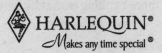